Pharaoh's Daughter

A NOVEL OF
ANCIENT EGYPT

JULIUS LESTER

HARPERTROPHY®
An Imprint of HarperCollins*Publishers*

Pharaoh's Daughter

 Printed in the United States of America. For information address HarperCollins Children's Books, a division of HarperCollins Publishers, 1350 Avenue of the Americas, New York, NY 10019.

This work was originally published in 2000 by Harcourt, Inc.
Published by arrangement with Harcourt, Inc.

Library of Congress Cataloging-in-Publication Data
Lester, Julius.
Pharaoh's daughter : a novel of ancient Egypt / by Julius Lester.
1st HarperTrophy ed.
p. cm.
Summary: A fictionalized account of the Biblical tale in which a Hebrew infant, rescued by the daughter of the Pharaoh, passes through a turbulent adolescence to eventually become a prophet of his people while his sister finds her true self as a priestess to the Egyptian gods.
ISBN 0-06-440969-4 (pbk.)
1. Egypt—Civilization—To 332 B.C.—Juvenile fiction. 2. Jews—History—to 1200 B.C.—Juvenile fiction. 3. Moses (Biblical leader)—Juvenile fiction. [1. Egypt—Civilization—To 332 B.C.—Fiction. 2. Jews—History—To 1200 B.C.—Fiction. 3. Moses (Biblical leader)—Fiction. 4. Bible. O.T.—History of Biblical events—Fiction. 5. Parent and child—Fiction.] I. Title.
PZ7.L5629 Ph 2002 2001024159
[Fic]—dc21

First Harper Trophy edition, 2002

Visit us on the World Wide Web!
www.harperchildrens.com

To
My Lady, Milan

Introduction

ONE QUESTION WRITERS are always asked is, "Where do you get your ideas?" I explain that fiction does not have its genesis in ideas but in feelings, and especially in a need to know something. I also explain that sometimes another person gives me an idea. So it was with this book.

Ms. Barbara Bader is a critic and librarian who reviewed a book of mine, *Sam and the Tigers,* for the *Horn Book,* the eminent journal of children's literature. Although we have never met, she called one afternoon to ask if I would undertake a picture-book retelling of the story of Moses, with Jerry Pinkney, who illustrated *Sam and the Tigers* and other books of mine.

Immediately I was reminded of Batya, the daughter of Pharaoh who finds the baby Moses in a basket in the river Nile and takes him to raise as her own son. In 1979, more than two years before I began studying for my eventual conversion to Judaism, I found myself spontaneously writing about this young woman for a lecture I was preparing for a class I taught then on Black-Jewish relations. Who was she? What motivated her to defy her father's orders that all Hebrew male babies were to be killed? I knew that the story I wanted to tell was too complex for a picture book, and thus this novel was born.

I wanted readers to experience Moses as a person. This is not easy because all of us have our associations with this figure, sometimes from religious school or films. It is difficult not to see Charlton Heston when one thinks of Moses. To free myself as writer from my own associations, I decided to spell Moses' name as Mosis, a shortened form of Tuthmosis. Mosis is a common suffix in ancient Egyptian, and often men were named for one of the many gods whose names carry that suffix. The suffix means "is born."

It seems that the writer of the Hebrew bible did not know that Mosis was the shortened form of an Egyptian name and associated it with the Hebrew verb *masha*, "to draw out." Thus, in the Hebrew bible, Pharaoh's daughter names the child Mosheh, "because I drew him out of the water." I have removed Moses from sacred history and have sought to put him into human history and thus thought it more accurate to spell his name as *Mosis* throughout this novel.

Writing this book became an experience that wholly involved me—intellectually, emotionally, spiritually. I became enthralled by ancient Egypt, a civilization that lasted some five thousand years and was probably as close to a paradise on earth as has ever been. But, more important, writing the novel became another journey into understanding who I was as I made the transition from my fifties and into my sixties. The courage to be who you are is something we learn and relearn throughout our decades, and perhaps that was why I had been drawn to the story of Pharaoh's daughter in 1979. Twenty years have passed and I am still learning who I am, still learning the courage to be.

YEAR 29 OF THE REIGN OF RAMESSES THE GREAT, 4TH MONTH OF SHEMU, DAY 28

Prologue

I SIT ON THE STONE BENCH in the garden of the Women's Palace. I have sat here almost every morning since I came to the palace fifteen years ago. Nothing has changed in all that time. The ibises wading in the lake could have been here when Ra'kha'ef built Hor-em-akhet a thousand years ago. In Khemet nothing changes. Past, present, and future merge and eternity is always now. At least that is how it was for me.

But I don't want to think about that. I want to sit here in peace, as I have every day after morning prayers. The baboons chatter quietly in the trees, their strenuous screeching to awaken Amon-Re, the sun god, finished for today. From inside the palace come faint sounds as the servants begin their morning chores. The white light of Amon-Re spreads farther and farther into the black sky. The god has survived another journey through the chaos of night.

Out of the corner of my eye, I notice someone come out of the palace. I turn to see who it is. I am surprised.

It is Batya, the oldest daughter of Pharaoh by his dead and still beloved wife, Queen Nefertari. Once Batya was called Meryetamun. For a while we were like sisters. Now we are not. However, there is respect. Sometimes that is better than love.

"Life, prosperity, and health!" I greet her in the usual way of Khemet.

"In peace, Almah," she returns weakly, not meeting my eyes.

Although we are no longer close, I know her well, and if Batya cannot look me in the eye, something is wrong. "What's the matter?"

"It's Mosis," she answers.

"Mosis? Has something happened to him?" I ask, getting to my feet, wanting to go to him.

Batya holds up a hand as if to restrain me. "He is not hurt. It is something else."

"Well, what?" I demand to know. "Tell me what is going on!" I am almost beside myself with worry and frustration. Why is she being so evasive?

"I would rather we were inside. Let me go to my suite. Wait a little and then join me there. It would be better if no one saw us going in together."

"Very well," I agree reluctantly, sitting down again. Why is she playing this game? Intrigue is not a part of Batya's nature. Something serious has happened. But what? Why doesn't she want anyone to see us together? Or is it that she wants to be certain that the just-returned Queen Asetnefret does not see us together? That must be it. Because I have not lived in the Women's Palace for many years, my being seen there would attract attention, and there is seldom a reward for being noticed by Asetnefret.

ENOUGH TIME HAS PASSED. And even if it hasn't, I can't wait any longer. I get up and, making sure no one is around, go casually but quickly into the palace and to the suite on the second floor where I lived with Batya when I first came here. No one has seen me. Without knocking I let myself in.

My brother sits on a couch, his head down. Batya is beside him. Although I see him every day, I still can't believe how much like a Khemetian he looks. The short wig fits his head as if he had been born into it. Even sitting, his height is apparent as well as his muscled torso and strong legs beneath the linen kilt. With the gray makeup around his eyes, he would look Khemetian to anyone who did not know, look as if he had been born into the house of Pharaoh.

Unfortunately this picture of Khemetian perfection is broken when Mosis speaks. There is no physical defect in his mouth and there are times when he gets so excited or angry that words pour out of his mouth like water from a fountain. But usually he speaks as if his tongue were as heavy as a stone in a pyramid.

"Mosis?" I say softly. "What is it?"

There is a long pause. He does not act as if he has heard me, though I know he has. Finally he says, "I murdered."

His head is down and the words are mumbled. I am not sure I heard what he said. "You did what?"

"I murdered."

His voice has the dull hollowness of footsteps in a tomb. I was not mistaken. That is what I heard the first time. I do not understand. I look from him to Batya, who holds his hands in hers. Mosis? My brother? Killed someone? "That—that doesn't make any sense," I say, bewildered, looking from one to the other. "What are you talking about?"

Mosis looks at Batya. She says, "I don't know. He will not tell me."

I still do not understand. Murder? In Khemet? That is unheard of. I go over and stoop down beside him. "Mosis," I say, taking his hands out of Batya's and holding them in mine. "What happened? What's going on? Please. Talk to me."

"Last night," Mosis answers.

"'Last night'? Yes. Go on."

He starts to cry.

"Kakemour," he whispers in a voice as dry as sand.

"What did you say?" I ask, feeling suddenly lightheaded.

"Kakemour," he repeats.

"You killed Kakemour?" I ask, panic rising in me at what this will mean.

He nods reluctantly.

"Why, Mosis?" I ask. "Why? What happened?"

Part One

YEAR 15 OF THE REIGN OF RAMESSES THE GREAT,
1ST MONTH OF AKHET

Chapter One

MY PARENTS TALKED in the darkness for a long time, their voices moving in and out of my sleep like the back of a hippopotamus rising and sinking in the Great Hapi. Abba, Father, spoke softly and slowly, while Ima, Mother, talked rapidly, as if she had to get all the words out before she forgot them. My brother Aharon, and sister, Miryam, are seven and four and hear nothing, not even the sounds of their own sleep. My baby brother, Yekutiel, is barely three months old. He sleeps through everything.

I am Almah, and I used to sleep like Yekutiel, but now that I am twelve I lie awake in the darkness. Something is wrong. Every evening after Abba comes home from working on the pharaoh's temple in Pi-Ramesses, men come to talk. My father is named Amram, and he is a leader of our people, the Habiru, "the people from the other side." ("The other side of what?" I asked him once. He said we have a land of our own, and one day our god, Ya, will send a redeemer who will lead us out of Khemet and into our land. Abba said that in our land the rivers flow with milk and honey. When I asked, "What is a redeemer and when is he coming?" he looked away.) Abba and the men talk long into the darkness, but their voices are low and I cannot hear their words. Yesterday I asked Ima what they were talking about. She looked at me as if I were bad luck that had come to life.

I get up when I see the blackness on the ceiling change to gray. Miryam has a leg on top of mine, an arm flung across my chest. Aharon lies pressed against me on the other side. Abba snores softly. Gently I move Miryam's arm and leg and get up. She and Aharon do not waken, but they sense I am leaving and move closer to each other. Aharon has only a little while longer to sleep before it will be time for him to get up and go with Abba to work in Pi-Ramesses.

Rubbing my eyes I walk into the kitchen and get the water jar. I go out the back door, past the bread oven built against the house, through the doorway in the wall, and into the narrow street. Pale pink tinges the eastern sky where the sun will rise.

Our house is on the corner of the Street of the Serpent and the Street of the River, at the farthest end of the village. It faces the Great Hapi, though at a safe distance. The river has started rising, which means the new year has begun. In Khemetian it is called the season of Akhet. The river will rise until it threatens to flow over the top of the road that protects us. That has never happened, though. But for almost two months it will be as if we are living next to the Great Green Sea. Then slowly, so slowly that we will not notice at first, the river will return to its bed and leave behind the thick black mud in which we will plant.

Other girls and women walk by me, water jars atop their heads like hair piled high, on their first of many trips to the river for water. Though one or two glance at me, they do not speak.

Instead of following them, I cross the street to a small path and disappear among the canebrake and the long sharp leaves of the papyri that tower above me. The birds send warning calls from the tops of the papyri. I would think they would know me by now.

Eventually I come to a stream, one of the branches of the Great Hapi where the river is not as wide or deep. The others are afraid to come here for water. Because of the snakes. They say I come here because I think I am better than anybody else and don't want to be around them. (*"Who cares if you can speak Khemetian? If you were a real Habiru, you would not speak the language of people who hate us."*) I tried to explain that it is quiet here and that I like the music of the silence and the music of the birds. They did not believe me. Perhaps because I was not telling the truth.

I look carefully for any snakes or crocodiles that might be hiding in the thick bulrushes. Then, looking around once more to be sure no one is watching, I take off my dress and face the sun. It seems to be reaching for me through the papyri as its warmth pours over my new-swelling breasts and the wispy hair that says I am becoming a woman.

This is the real reason I come here for water. I have never told anyone. It is my secret. Mine and the sun's. I raise my arms high over my head and move them outward in a circle as if I am holding the sun, but it does not burn me because I love it and it loves me. I close my eyes and tongues of warmth cover my body. I think I could stand here like this for the rest of my life.

However, sooner than I would like, I get nervous that someone will see me. I know they can't, but that does not matter. I force my eyes open and slip my dress on. Then I fill the jar, put it on my head, and start for home.

When I reach the kitchen, I pour the water into a larger jug. I will carry water from the river many times today until the big jug is filled. Now, however, I take the bread, cucumbers, and dried fish from the baskets where they are kept, slice them, and put them on a reed plate. Then, filling a bowl with water, I go up the stairs to the roof, where Abba is kneeling and facing the sun.

Each morning, when he hears me go out to get water Abba gets up. He likes to begin the day praising and thanking Ya. It looks as if he is praying to the sun, but the Habiru are not like Khemetians, who say the sun is a god named Amon-Re. Abba says the sun is a light in the sky that Ya made.

I put Abba's breakfast down. His eyes are closed and his lips move rapidly, but I cannot hear any words. I squat nearby and wait.

Before long Abba opens his eyes, turns, and smiles at me. "Good morning, Almah."

"Good morning, Abba."

I hand him his breakfast. He sits down opposite me

and crosses his legs, his back to the sun. "We must talk, Almah," he begins, tearing off a piece of bread and putting it in his mouth.

His voice is quiet and serious. I am scared, wondering what I did wrong.

"How old are you now?"

"Twelve." Why is he asking me something he knows the answer to?

He nods. "You are almost a woman." He bites into a slice of cucumber.

Now I know what this is about—he has chosen a husband for me. I don't care who it is. I won't marry him or anybody, not now. Not ever!

"Ima and I need your help." His face is almost mournful.

What is the matter? Is he sick? Ima? What is wrong? "What do you want me to do, Abba?" I ask, afraid to hear the answer.

He smiles, but his smile is weak, like the moon on the nights when it is shrinking. He drinks deeply from the bowl of water. With his long hair and big dark beard, I imagine that Ya looks like Abba. (Ima said, "Ya does not look like anything, and certainly not like a man.") He is big and his muscles are as hard as sun-dried bricks because he helps move the heavy stones for the temple. But his eyes are soft and kind. Not like Ima's.

"I'm sure you have been wondering why all the men have been coming to our house in the evenings and what Ima and I talk about late into the night."

Of course! All those men have sons, and Abba and Ima have been whispering in the night trying to decide which one I should marry. I would rather die!

"This is not easy to talk about," Abba continues. "I find it hard to believe myself." He is speaking Khemetian now. He does this when he wants to make me feel that I am special to him. Since before I can remember, Abba has spoken to me in Khemetian, which he learned when he started working in Pi-Ramesses as a boy. When I used to go to the market there with Ima, I interpreted for her and many of the other Habiru women. But they still don't like me. ("Khemetian is the language of people who hate Ya," Ima says. Abba says it is the language of the people we live among: "We should know what they are saying and be able to talk to them." Ima is afraid that if I speak Khemetian I will become one. That is what she says. I think she doesn't like that Abba and I can talk and she doesn't know what we're saying.)

"There is a rumor that Pharaoh is going to have all newborn Habiru baby boys killed."

I do not understand. Is that what all the whispering and talking has been about? I am relieved but a little disappointed, too. I am old enough to marry. Even if I don't want to, why hasn't someone come and asked Abba for me? "That doesn't make sense," I say aloud. "Why would the pharaoh want to kill all the baby boys?"

Abba shakes his head. "Perhaps because we do not worship him as the other foreigners in Khemet do. Ya says we must worship only him and none other. Maybe that is why Pharaoh dislikes us. I do not know, Almah.

Who am I to understand the mind of Ramesses? But the *why* does not matter. If the rumor is true, we must make sure his soldiers do not find your little brother, or anyone else's. This is why Ima and I are going to need you more than ever."

"What do you want me to do?" I ask seriously.

"To watch out for the soldiers so they don't surprise us."

I want to help, but since Yekutiel was born, I have been doing a lot of the work Ima always did. "How can I do that and also get water, grind the grain and make bread, weave baskets, dishes, and cloth?" I complain.

"I know. This is more important. Your mother will manage," he reassures me. "We need you to keep a lookout. You won't be alone. All the girls who are not married will also be watching."

"What do I do if I see any soldiers?"

"Run to as many houses as you can and warn people so they can hide the babies."

"But where will they hide them?"

"In baskets, which they will put among the canes and bulrushes and cattails along the banks of the river."

"When do I start?"

"Today. We do not know when the soldiers are coming. Or if they are coming. But we must be ready."

AT FIRST IT IS EXCITING. Children run this way and that through the streets, looking for soldiers. But by the time the sun reaches the top of the sky, the smaller ones are tired and bored and are playing more than they are looking. By the next day, and certainly the one after, even many of the girls my age are doing more talking and giggling than looking.

A few days later, just as I think Abba is mistaken about the soldiers, I am standing in the road and there in the distance, where the broad paved road of Pi-Ramesses changes to the narrow dirt one of Goshen, I see figures. The only time so many people would be coming to Goshen is when the men come back from working in Pi-Ramesses, and it is too early for that. I run down the road until I can see them clearly. Soldiers! They walk two by two, the sunlight flashing off their upright spears like a warning. Wearing only loincloths, their bodies look so powerful, as if they will kill us with the mere appearance of their muscles.

I run back up the road as fast as I can and am almost out of breath when I burst into the house. "Ima! Ima! Soldiers! We must hurry!"

Ima comes out of the middle room, where we sleep. Sucking her thumb, Miryam is clutching Ima's skirt. Ima puts her finger to her lips, asking me to be quiet so as not to wake Yekutiel, as if anything could. "Where are they?"

"Just crossing into Goshen."

"Go back and keep watch. They may not come this far today."

I hurry back. I do not see any soldiers now. Where did they go? All I see is a lone figure in the distance. I don't hear any sounds from the village, either, but I do see an occasional figure run across the road and down the embankment to the river, carrying a basket and then returning with empty arms.

I continue looking for the soldiers. Only when I am almost out of Goshen do I see them at the far end of the Street of Avraham, going in and out of houses. They do not seem to be in a hurry. I hide on the riverbank just below the road to watch. Glancing up and down the river, I can see baskets among the thick stalks of the bulrushes and papyrus plants. But I see them only because I know what to look for. The soldiers will not see anything except bulrushes and papyri.

I see two soldiers on a rooftop. One holds a struggling woman while the other shoves his spear through a closed basket. The woman screams so loud I am surprised the river does not rise up to see what is wrong.

I . . . I do not want to see any more. I get up to go and, a short distance away, see a woman staring into the river. It must be the figure I saw earlier.

I have never seen anyone so beautiful. Her hair is plaited in many long tight braids that look like strands of night as they stream onto her shoulders and down her back. From beneath her hair large golden earrings flash like sunlight on the water. Around her head is a band of blue and red stones, and she has on a necklace like her headband; but these stones are larger, each one surrounded by a strip of gold, and it lies against her chest like the curve of the sun. Her eyes are large and the upper eyelids are painted dark gray, while the lower lids are painted dark green. The two colors meet at the corners of her eyes and extend outward in a line that goes almost as far back as her hair. Her lips are painted red, as if she took the color from the setting sun. I wonder if she is a goddess.

What is she doing here? Is she lost? I wonder if I should ask her, but it is none of my business. Then, just as I am about to turn away, I see her body tense. She is looking at something in the water. Suddenly she puts the back of her hand against her lips and opens her mouth, but no sound comes out. Instead she slumps to the ground as if a ray of sun has pierced her heart into stillness.

Without thinking I run up the embankment and onto the road. When I reach her I look down into the water. It is red. Green and white pieces of a basket float on the water, and I see the round bulging eyes of a crocodile as it disappears into the dark, bloody coldness.

Chapter Two

I WANT TO GO BACK TO BED and give this day a chance to start over again and be better. But the Khemetian woman's eyes flutter open slowly and get big when she sees me.

"It's—it's all right," I say in Khemetian.

She frowns. "You are Habiru?"

"Yes."

She shakes her head slowly, as if this is a bad dream from which she must awake. Where else would a Habiru girl be speaking Khemetian? With effort she sits up. "I . . . I must go. I should not be here. I am Princess Meryetamun. I am Pharaoh's daughter."

Now *my* eyes grow large. I was right. She *is* a goddess. If the pharaoh is a god, would not his daughter be a goddess? But the pharaoh is not a god. Ya is. But what if the pharaoh really is a god? Should I bow? No. Ya might kill me. Or Ima.

"Which way is Pi-Ramesses?"

That is when I know she is not well. Pi-Ramesses is in

the direction she is looking. "Would the princess like to come to my house and rest for a while?"

"No!" she exclaims. "I asked you a question. Which direction is Pi-Ramesses?"

I point. She looks. Then she turns in the other direction. "I am confused," she admits; her voice is small and weak now. She starts to stand up. I offer my hand but she ignores it. The princess is almost to her feet when her knees give way and she slumps to the ground again.

I do not know what to do. I want to get help but am afraid to leave her. Crocodiles move on land as easily and as quickly as they swim in the river. Sometimes they walk along this road as if going to work in Pi-Ramesses.

"A little water, perhaps," I suggest.

"Yes. Yes. That would be good," she admits. Her face is as white as the moon's on a night when it shines like the sun.

She gets up slowly. I offer my hand again.

"No one is allowed to touch the pharaoh or a member of his family," she says. "The penalty for doing so is death."

I am not sure I heard her correctly. "I am sorry, Princess. Could you repeat what you said . . . slowly?"

She does so, and I say again to myself in Habiru to make sure I understand. I do. So, whenever she stumbles and almost loses her balance, I do not try to catch her. Eventually we reach our house.

"Ima! Ima!" I call excitedly as the princess walks unsteadily inside and slumps to the floor.

Ima comes hurrying from the other room, Yekutiel in

her arms, Miryam hiding behind her legs. Ima is startled to see the Khemetian woman and shoves Yekutiel into Miryam's arms, then pushes her out of sight. Quickly I tell Ima everything that happened and who the woman is.

"You fool!" Ima snaps when I am finished. "You were supposed to warn me when the soldiers were coming. Instead you bring Pharaoh's own daughter into our house! What were you thinking?"

I . . . I do not know what to say. Ima is right; I did not think. But looking at the princess sitting on the reed-matted floor, like a little girl who needs her mother, I do not know what else I was supposed to have done.

"Well, now that she is here, perhaps a little kindness from us will lead her to seek kindness for us from her father, the butcher of children! Get her some water."

I run to the kitchen and return quickly with a pitcher and bowl. I fill the bowl and hand it to the princess. She does not notice.

"Princess?" I say softly.

She blinks her eyes, and it is as if she wakes up and sees where she is for the first time. I notice that Ima has gone into the middle room. "What is your name?" the princess asks.

"Almah."

"Thank you, Almah," she says, taking the bowl from me and drinking. When she is finished I refill the bowl. She empties it. I fill it again and this time she drinks more slowly. Finally she puts the bowl on the floor and looks around.

I am ashamed as I look at my home and myself

through her eyes. It is a dark and narrow room, with only a little light coming in through the small oblong windows near the ceiling. The mud-brick walls are bare, and the only furniture is the low table on which we put the food when we eat. The reed mats covering the floor are worn. If I did not have to be out looking for soldiers, I would be gathering reeds to make new ones. And what must I look like to her—a thin female, no longer a child, not yet a woman, with black curly hair and eyes as dark as mud. Sometimes I look at my face when getting water from the river, and my lips are too full and my nose too narrow for me to be pretty. But if I were ugly, at least one girl in the village would have been glad to tell me by now. Perhaps it is worse than I think, since no one has ever told me that I am pretty or ugly. No one except Abba, who says I am beautiful.

"How are you feeling?" I ask, not wanting her to think anymore about how this room or I look.

"Better," she says.

It is true. Her face is not so pale.

Just then the door opens. It is Abba and Aharon. When my brother sees the princess, his eyes get large, like hers when she saw me. Aharon looks up at Abba, then runs from the room.

Abba's eyes narrow as he looks from the princess to me. Before he can wonder if Yekutiel is safe, I tell him in Habiru what happened and the tension leaves his face.

Abba turns to the princess. "I am Amram," he introduces himself in Khemetian.

"I am Meryetamun, the daughter of Pharaoh."

"My daughter explained to me that you were not feeling well and needed to rest. Welcome to our home."

"Thank you. Your Khemetian is nearly perfect."

"You flatter me. I learned your language some years ago, as a boy, when I began working in Pi-Ramesses. May we offer you something to eat? Some fruit? Grapes? Apples?"

"Grapes would be delicious. Perhaps I am more hungry than anything else."

I hurry back to the kitchen and return with a basket of grapes.

The princess eats slowly. "Almah?" she asks after a while.

"Yes, Princess?"

"When you found me this afternoon, did . . . did you see anything?"

I know what she is asking. What should I say? I want to look at Abba. He would know how to answer. But the princess is looking directly at me. "'See anything'?" I repeat.

"In the water. Did you see anything?"

"Such as?"

"A basket, perhaps?"

I feel Abba looking at me and I know I must not tell her the truth. She wants to know how we are hiding the babies so she can tell the soldiers what to look for. "Did the princess lose something in the river?"

"Never mind," she says abruptly. I cannot tell if she thinks I am stupid or lying.

Suddenly, from the other room Yekutiel lets out a squeal that is quickly muffled.

"Was that a baby? Didn't I see a baby when I came in?" the princess asks.

"I heard nothing," Abba says.

The princess gets to her feet. Now she looks like one who could tell the sun to stop shining and it would obey. "Almah. Your mother was standing there, holding a baby, when I first came in."

"The sun will be down soon, Princess," Abba says quietly but firmly. "Everyone at the palace must be concerned about the daughter of Pharaoh. Isn't it unusual for the Royal Daughter to be in Goshen among the Habiru? And without servants? I would not want your father, Lord of the Two Lands and the Bringer of Light, to think unkind thoughts because his daughter ventured unbidden into our village. Almah will walk back with you so you will not lose your way."

Abba's voice is smooth, like lotion, and I can see the princess becoming soft beneath his words.

"You speak well, Amram," she says, smiling slightly. "I . . . I did not mean any harm to your wife—or your baby. I only wanted to see the child."

"If there were a child to see, Princess, it would have been our honor to show her to you."

I start to say the baby is a him but realize in time that Abba does not want the princess to know the truth.

It is late afternoon as the princess and I leave. Many people walk along the road as the workers return from Pi-Ramesses. Everyone stares at us. Some recognize me, and I hear them whispering, "Isn't that the daughter of Amram? Of course she would be with a Khemetian!"

Walking next to the princess with everyone looking at us, I feel something I have never felt in my life. I feel important.

"How old are you, Almah?" the princess asks me.

"Twelve."

"You seem older. I would have thought you were at least my age, but I can see now that your breasts are only beginning."

"May I ask how old you are, Princess?"

"Fifteen."

She is a woman. "You are married?" I ask her.

She looks down at me. "Why do you ask?"

I don't know what to say. Most girls are married by the time they are twelve. But maybe it is different if you are a princess. "I wanted to know what it is like to be married," I say finally.

"I don't know. There is someone who would marry me, but I don't think I want to marry him—or anyone."

"Me, too!" I exclaim excitedly. "Me, too!"

She laughs. I do not know what is so funny, but I am pleased that I made her laugh.

"And why would you not want to marry?" she asks me.

"I just don't."

She laughs again, but this time it is quieter. "That's probably the best reason there is. But don't you want to have children?"

I start to tell her how much I took care of Aharon when he was little, and Miryam and Yekutiel now, but I stop myself. "I'm not sure."

"If you do not have children, what will happen to you?"

I do not understand. "What do you mean?"

"What do the Habiru do to women who do not have children?"

I still do not understand. "Nothing. I mean, I don't know. Why would someone do something to you because you didn't have a child?"

"Among my people, having children is so important that some men kill themselves if they do not become fathers. A woman who does not have a child is called Mother of the Absent One."

I do not want to be anyone's mother, present or absent.

Ahead of us I see the entrance to Pi-Ramesses. The inscribed pylons rise high into the sky to form a gateway. On each side are two huge statues of the pharaoh sitting in a chair as if he is judging every person who passes. This is the Avenue of the Pharaoh, and as we pass beneath the pylon, the road widens and is now made of large stones. On both sides huge statues hover as far as I can see. Some are lions with the faces of men. Others are men with the heads of rams, or birds and women balancing the sun on their heads between two curved horns. Mostly, though, there are huge statues of the pharaoh, these of him standing, his left leg forward. I should go back now, but it has been so long since I was last here.

Before Yekutiel was born, I would come to the market with Ima to swap vegetables and baskets for grain, fruit, and flax. Women still come to the house and ask Ima if I can go to market with them. They get more when I do the bargaining because I speak Khemetian, but Ima won't let me go with them. She is afraid of what I might learn or do if I go to Pi-Ramesses without her.

She is right. Whenever my bare feet touched the stones of Pi-Ramesses, I felt safer than when I walked in the dust and dirt of Goshen. I also liked looking at the statues of Khemetian gods. I wanted to know their names, what they did, and why the statues were so huge. Ima didn't want me to look at them. (*"How can people be so foolish as to worship a man with the head of a bird?"*) I thought it was easier to believe in a god that looked kind of like something you knew than one you couldn't see.

I would love to come into the city and go anywhere I wanted. I don't even know how big Pi-Ramesses is. Abba said it is divided into four sections, each one dedicated to a different god or goddess. Each has its own temple where the priests do rituals. In the center is the main temple, the one Abba and Aharon are helping build. The marketplace is outside that temple. I have never seen anything like it. It has columns so tall I cannot see their tops. And the columns are so big around that if two men with long arms stood on each side and put their arms around one, their fingertips would not meet. From here I can just see the golden dome of the main temple shining like the sun when it is at the top of the sky.

In every direction there are buildings, mostly houses. Grain is stored in the larger ones, Abba told me. During the day the street is crowded with people and animals carrying goods from the boats docked at the wharf, which I see in the distance to my right. Now, however, it is late and there are not many people about.

We come to another street. I really should turn back. But what if the princess starts to feel faint again? And if the princess didn't want me to come this far, she would have said something. So, she must want me to stay with her until she is home safely. I follow the princess along a street that is even broader than the Avenue of the Pharaoh. The stones here are very smooth, almost like glass. They are painted red, white, and green. On either side are date and palm and sycamore trees, grass as smooth as the river at the Season of the Inundation, and statues of the pharaoh leading to a long white wall stretching farther than I can see. The sun shines brightly off the gold-domed roof of a building behind the walls.

"That is the pharaoh's palace," the princess tells me, pointing at the golden dome.

I follow her until we stop before two large doors on which are painted a lotus and a papyrus plant in white, blue, and green.

"Come in," says the princess. "The sun will be going down soon. You could stay here in the palace tonight and return home in the morning. I could show you around the Women's Palace and the main palace where the pharaoh lives."

"The women have their own separate palace?" I ask, amazed.

The princess smiles. "Come. Let me show you."

I want so much to say yes, but I shake my head. "Ima and Abba would worry." Then I remember: She is Pharaoh's daughter. Her father wants to kill my brother. But she seems so nice. I start to walk away, but I start crying. I want to stay in the palace with her because I like her and wish I could be like her and Ima will be angry at me for bringing her to our house and I wish I didn't like her and I wish the sun wasn't as red as a baby's blood.

I stop. When I turn around she is staring after me and I want to run to her. Instead I yell, "There were pieces of straw scattered all over the water! And there was blood, lots and lots and lots of blood!" And I run away as fast as I can, tears streaming down my face.

Chapter Three

WHEN I GET HOME the front room is filled with men sitting on the floor who start shouting at me as soon as I walk in.

"What did she say?"

"Tell us. Tell us. Is she going to send the army?"

I do not understand what they are talking about or why they are shouting at me as if I have done something wrong. I am too old to cry and I am afraid I might, but just then I feel a hand on my shoulder. Abba! I wish he would pick me up and hold me like he does Miryam, like he used to hold me. Instead he raises his arms and everyone quiets.

"So, my daughter," he begins, smiling at me. "It is not every day that one of us talks with the daughter of Pharaoh. Everyone is eager to know what she said."

"About what?" I ask.

Abba chuckles. "About anything."

I would tell Abba everything but I don't want these other men to know. It was private, a conversation between two women. "We didn't talk much."

"Did she ask you any questions? Questions about us?" someone asks anxiously.

I shake my head. "No."

"No?" many voices respond, as if they don't believe me.

"Quiet!" Abba orders. "Go on, Almah."

"We didn't talk much. She wanted me to spend the night at the palace and said she would show me everything, but I told her that you and Ima would worry about me." I stop abruptly.

"Go on! Go on!" come the cries.

I look up at Abba, hoping he will tell me that I don't have to tell them more, but he says, "Is there something else, Almah? It is important that we know."

"I told her about the crocodile that killed the baby this afternoon," I continue, looking only at him, "and about all the blood that was on the water and how I didn't know a little baby was filled with so much blood, Abba."

There are gasps of shock and surprise. When it is quiet again, Abba asks, "And what did the princess say?"

"I . . . I . . . I don't know, Abba. I was angry and I was afraid and I ran." My voice is small. I bury my face against him and he puts an arm around me.

"This is outrageous!" someone exclaims. "Because of an impudent brat, we're all going to be killed!"

There is much shouting and talking, and I want to cover my ears. Why are they angry at me? I didn't do anything!

Abba raises his arms again and everyone is quiet. "Now, gentlemen," he says in a loud voice, "let us not get carried away by fear. The princess could have asked my daughter any question she wanted about where we were hiding the children, and she did not. What more proof do you want that she did not come here to spy on us?"

The shouting and yelling begin again. I am very tired and sleepy, and I slip into the middle room to look for Ima, but she isn't there. I find her and the children on the roof. She is sitting facing the doorway I've just come through. Aharon, Miryam, and Yekutiel are asleep beside her.

"Ima?" I say softly. As I get closer I can see that she is looking at me as if I do not belong to her.

I go to lie down between Aharon and Miryam as always.

"Are you trying to wake them up?" Ima hisses. She moves her arm angrily, as if shooing away a mosquito. I don't know what to do. Her arm sweeps out again as if knocking flies off carrots. I go to the far edge of the roof and lie down. What did I do to her? If I had known she would be angry at me even though I didn't stay at the Women's Palace, I would have stayed.

I don't remember falling asleep, but I am awakened by loud shouting from inside the house. It is Abba and Ima! I . . . I can't believe it. I have never heard them yell at each other. Then I hear my name. They are fighting about me! Ima is doing most of the shouting. I put my hands over my ears and close my eyes tightly. The next thing I know, my eyes open just as the sky is changing from black to gray.

I sit up and look around. I am alone on the roof. Then I remember Abba and Ima shouting at each other about me and I feel sick in my stomach. I don't want to get up. I don't want to go inside. But already I hear doors opening and closing from other houses and the soft fall of feet on the dirt street.

I go down the stairs quietly. I do not want them to hear me: I do not want them to know I am alive. But I hear them talking softly. Have they been awake all night talking about me?

"I am afraid." Ima's voice trembles as if she is about to cry.

"She is a good daughter. Almah works as hard as any girl in the village. Harder! Whatever you ask her to do, she does. And she never complains."

"I know. I know. But she frightens me."

"What do you mean?"

"Yesterday. Did you see?"

"See what?"

"She was not afraid, Amram. She was not afraid of the princess."

"And that frightens you? I don't understand."

"Don't you see? Any other girl in this village would have left a wealthy-looking Khemetian woman lying in the road, and run home and told her mother. No Habiru girl would have brought a Khemetian into her home without permission. But it did not occur to Almah that she had done something wrong. Even now she doesn't think she made a mistake. That is what frightens me."

"But isn't that what Ya wants us to do? Haven't we taught her to care about others? Haven't we taught her that she should be afraid of no one except Ya?"

"Yes. Yes."

"Then, what?"

There is a long silence. Finally I hear Ima say, "Maybe if you had not taught her Khemetian . . . But she is more your daughter than mine, anyway," she says, her voice aching with hurt.

Abba laughs uncomfortably. "That is not true, Yocheved." *But it is, Abba,* I say silently. "I did not set out to teach her Khemetian. It just happened. She took to the language so readily. And I've been thinking, what Almah did yesterday might save us."

Abba's voice drops to a whisper and I can no longer hear. Quietly, I go back up the stairs to the roof. There is a broad arc of white on the horizon at the place where the sun will rise. In the distance baboons are shrieking. The Khemetians believe the cries of the baboons awaken Amon-Re, the sun god. I wish they would let him sleep this morning. I don't want another day like yesterday. I thought I was doing the right thing. There wasn't time to be afraid or run home and ask Ima what I should do.

Then I realize: Ima cannot know what I should have done. She was not there. She did not see the crocodile's round eyes, the bits of basket floating on the bloody water. She did not see the princess fall to the earth as if she were dead. I did. Just because she is my mother, it does not mean she is always right.

I hear footsteps. It is Abba.

"Good morning." He smiles.

I do not smile back. "I'm sorry I overslept. I will get your breakfast and then go for water."

As I start to move past him, he puts out an arm and stops me. "What's the matter, Almah?"

His voice is soft and he looks worried. My bottom lip starts to tremble. I am going to cry and I don't want to. "Ima wasn't there, Abba. She can't know what I should have done." I say it in Khemetian so, if she is listening, she won't understand. The tears roll down my face, but I choke back any sound because I am afraid that what will come out will not be sobs but screams. I am so angry and so sad.

Abba pulls me to him and hugs me tightly to his chest, and now the sounds come but they are soft cries. "Why does Ima hate me, Abba?" I ask in a voice as tiny as a grain of sand.

"Oh, Almah! Your mother doesn't hate you. Don't ever think that! I know she is harsh with you sometimes. But that is because she loves you so much."

"No she doesn't, Abba," I answer, unafraid of what I am saying.

Abba takes my hand and we walk to the edge of the roof overlooking the street and sit, our backs against the wall. "Your mother does not see yet that you are almost a woman, that we will be finding a husband for you soon. She misses her little girl."

"That's not it, Abba. She doesn't like me because I know things she doesn't. She doesn't like me because I'm not like her. I'm different."

Abba blushes and tries to laugh. That's what adults do when they don't know what to say. "That is not so," he answers, but nothing in his voice makes me believe him.

"We will talk about this more at another time. Right now there is something else I need to talk with you about."

I wipe my eyes and look up at him.

"I need to know what else you and the princess talked about on your walk back to the palace. You were not telling everything."

"It was—well, you know—just something that girls talk about."

Abba smiles. "Oh, really? Like sisters?"

"Yes! *That's it!*" I exclaim, understanding now why I feel close to her. "She wanted to know how old I am. She's fifteen, but she's not married and she said she doesn't want to get married and I told her I didn't either. And then she wanted to know what will happen to me if I don't get married and have children. I didn't understand, but she said that Khemetians have to have children or they are called bad names. Abba, did you know that the princess lives in a separate palace called the Women's Palace?"

"No, I didn't. Would you like to live in a place that was just for women?"

"Maybe," I answer.

"Well, the next time you see the princess, if she asks to show you the Women's Palace, it would be all right with me if you went."

"Really?"

"Really."

My excitement dwindles quickly, though, as I remember the last thing I said to her. "I'll never see the princess again. Not after what I said to her."

"Don't be sure. I have a feeling the princess is going to come looking for you. If you need a big sister, she might need a little one. You and I like the princess and trust her. Everyone else thinks she came to spy on us. Your mother thinks she may have been pretending to be ill to get inside one of our homes. Ima even wonders if the pharaoh knows I am a leader of our people and sent her to find where we live."

"What do you think, Abba?"

"I believe Ya sent her and he also sent you to her."

"He *did*?"

He nods. "I think he did. Usually it is Ima who seems to know what Ya wants. But ever since you were little and I saw how quickly you learned Khemetian, I have wondered if Ya did not have a plan for you. When I came in yesterday and saw you and the princess, the first thought that came to me was that this was part of Ya's plan. So I want you to watch for the princess."

"Is she coming back?" I ask, excited.

"I think so."

"And if I see her, what should I do?"

Abba smiles. "I do not know, Almah. But *you* will."

Chapter Four

THE SOLDIERS RETURN each morning and begin searching at the house where they stopped the evening before. Because we know where they are going, we don't need to watch for them.

Instead I look for the princess. After getting water I walk toward Pi-Ramesses until I see the walls that surround the palace shining white in the sun like herons' wings. I think that somehow she will know I am there and come walking out. But she never does.

One morning on my way to stare at the white walls, I pass a small group of soldiers as they are about to start down another street. I pay them no attention. They must know by now that they are not going to find what they are looking for, especially since we know where they are going to search each day. Since that first day, neither they nor the crocodiles have found any children.

The soldiers have almost passed me, when suddenly, "You!"

I am startled and stop immediately. What have I done

now? I turn around slowly and am surprised to see a soldier smiling at me.

"Was it you I saw with Princess Meryetamun?" he asks me in Habiru. He speaks slowly and his accent is not very good.

I do not know what to say. Where did he see me with the princess? In Pi-Ramesses, or did the princess describe me to the soldiers and tell them to look for the girl who had insulted her? What am I supposed to do?

I look at him. Like all the soldiers, his chest is bare and gleams with a sweet-smelling oil, which shows off the hard muscles in his arms, shoulders, chest, and the smooth bare legs beneath his kilt. His eyes are painted gray and his hair is short.

"Yes," I say in Khemetian.

He looks as if he wants to ask me something but doesn't know if he should.

"What's your name?" He is still speaking Habiru.

"Almah."

"That's pretty."

"Thank you. What is your name?" I respond in Khemetian.

"Kakemour." Then he chuckles. "You speak Khemetian like a Khemetian," he says in his own language this time. "I speak Habiru like a Khemetian." He laughs.

I laugh with him.

"Do you think you will be seeing the princess again?" he asks suddenly.

I am surprised. Why is he asking me that? I start to say no, but then I remember what Abba said. "Maybe."

"Well, if you do, tell her that Kakemour said—" He stops. "Never mind."

I want to ask him what he was going to say. Then I blurt out, "Are you the one who wants to marry her?"

"How did you know? What did she say?" His voice is excited and eager. He laughs nervously.

"She said that she doesn't want to marry anyone. I don't, either," I add proudly.

Kakemour smiles sadly. "If she would say that to a stranger, then it must be true." He speaks softly as if he is talking to himself. Then, without another word, he turns and hurries to catch up with the rest of the soldiers.

The next morning I awake as usual when the black of the sky is turning gray. Since the night Ima left me on the roof to sleep alone, I have slept here. I don't want to be in the same room with her. Although I miss having Miryam and Aharon snuggle against me, Ima does not want them near me anymore.

I get up, and as I stretch I happen to look toward Pi-Ramesses, when I see them! Hundreds of soldiers running fast up the road.

I almost fall down the stairs. "Abba! Ima! Soldiers! Hundreds of them!" I do not wait for them to answer but grab Yekutiel's basket and take him from where he lies beside Ima. Aharon and Miryam awake and look at me curiously.

"What are you doing?" Ima says, reaching out for the baby.

I move away from her.

"Go, Almah! Quickly!" Abba says.

I run into the kitchen with Yekutiel and grab some bread and dates and am through the door, the sound of Ima wailing in my ears. I think I hear Abba right behind me, hurrying to warn as many of our neighbors as he can. The soldiers tricked us into thinking that they didn't care about finding any babies.

I hurry down the path to the river. Yekutiel has not made a sound, but he is strange that way. He almost never cries. Sometimes we wonder if there is something wrong with his voice.

When I reach the river, I settle myself at the lip of the embankment, where I can see the soldiers long before they see me. If I do see any, I'll put Yekutiel in the basket and hide it among the bulrushes. They are thick here and the basket is made of them. No one will ever find it unless he is looking for it. I hope.

For now I lay Yekutiel on my lap, facing me, his head resting lightly on my knees. The sun's warmth spreads over us. I would think it is a beautiful day if I couldn't hear the faint sounds of screaming and crying.

I hear someone coming and quickly put the baby in the basket, which is already hidden in the bulrushes. I scurry around a curve in the riverbank where I can hide and wait to see who it is. In a short while someone appears. It is Ima. She is looking frantically this way and that.

I stand up and hurry to her. "Ima!" I call, but quietly so only she can hear me.

"Almah! The baby! Where is he? I came to feed him."

When Ima sees how cleverly I hid the basket, she smiles at me. "You did well. Even I did not see it there."

I smile. I wish she said nice things to me more often.

She nurses him and then hurries back to the village. Yekutiel will sleep for many hours now.

The sun moves up the sky until it is directly overhead. I eat the bread and the dates I took as I hurried out. It is quiet now. I have not heard any crying and screaming from the village in a long while. I wonder if I can go back but decide to stay until Abba or Ima comes to get me.

Occasionally ducks land on the water and look at me. When they fly away I fear they are going to tell the soldiers where to find a Habiru baby.

The sun has started its downward journey when I hear someone coming. It is probably Ima coming to feed Yekutiel again, but I can't take any chances. I look quickly at the basket to be sure it is well hidden, then hurry to my hiding place around the curve of the river.

From the noise made by the leaves being brushed, I can tell there is more than one person. It must be soldiers! The sounds come closer and closer, and I cannot believe who steps into the clearing. The princess! It can't be! But it is. She looks different today. I do not know why until I notice that she is not wearing jewelry and, thus, does not sparkle in the sun. She is still beautiful. Behind her are two girls about my age who must be servants, because they are not wearing clothes.

The princess stands on the bank peering intently into the water. Suddenly she points. Oh no! She is pointing at the basket. How did she find it? Even Ima didn't see it. But the princess acted as if she knew where it was all along. But she couldn't have known. She couldn't have! What am I going to do?

I can hear her voice, but she is speaking so fast I do not understand a word. She is angry, though, and grabs one of the girls by the throat and then pushes her down. Both girls scramble down the embankment, get the basket, and set it at the princess's feet. She opens it. She is picking my brother up. I don't believe it. He is lying in her arms as if . . . as if . . . as if she is me or Ima. His head turns toward her breast and his little mouth puckers, moving back and forth. Then I see his mouth open as if he is going to cry out, and I spring up from my hiding place.

"Would the princess like my mother to nurse the child for her?" I call.

The princess turns. "Almah?" she exclaims. "Is this your brother? The one I thought I saw when I was at your house?"

What can I say? "Yes, Princess."

"Do not worry. He is safe with me. Taweret has given him to me."

"'Taweret'?"

"She is the goddess who brings babies to women who are childless, as I am."

"But . . . but he is not yours," I say.

"He is unless you want the soldiers to kill him as they have killed so many today. Take me to your mother. The baby is hungry."

I feel sick. I have failed again. I saved my brother from the soldiers, but the princess says he is hers now. Abba and Ima will never trust me again.

Chapter Five

THE SOLDIERS ARE JUST entering my house when we come out of the marsh—the princess, her two servants, and me. Standing beside the door, Aharon and Miryam next to them, Abba's and Ima's eyes swell with fear as they see Yekutiel being carried by the princess. But as we come closer and they see how Yekutiel is making sounds at the princess and giggling when she tickles him under his chin, the fear is replaced by confusion. I am neither afraid nor confused. Just jealous. How dare he!

When the soldiers see the princess, they drop to their knees and bow. The only one who doesn't is the soldier who asked me about her yesterday: Kakemour.

"Meryetamun?" he asks, astonished to see her.

"Kakemour." The princess seems almost as surprised.

"I . . . I don't understand. What . . . what are you doing here?"

"The goddess Taweret has given me a child, as I'm sure you can see."

Kakemour frowns. "Be that as it may, you have placed

my men in an impossible position. How can we carry out the pharaoh's orders when his own daughter disobeys them? You are going against *maat*, 'divine order.'"

"How can I be going against *maat* when the goddess herself delivered this child into my hands?" the princess responds evenly.

Kakemour doesn't know what to say, and before he can think of anything, Yekutiel starts crying. Ima hurries to the princess and takes the baby from her. That only seems to make him cry harder and his tiny arms reach back for the princess as Ima takes him inside to nurse.

"Have you lost your mind?" Kakemour says to the princess, openly annoyed now.

"Do you know to whom you are speaking?" the princess replies sharply, her eyes narrowing. "You may be the son of Intef, the *tjat*, prime minister, to Pharaoh, and the future *tjat*, but even then I will be Meryetamun, daughter of Ramesses the Great!"

Kakemour turns red and bows. "Forgive me, Princess, favorite daughter of the Lord of the Two Lands, son of Amon-Re." His voice is sarcastic, then it softens as he says, "I thought you were Meryetamun, my oldest friend, my dearest friend, and the woman I want to marry."

Their voices are quiet, but I can still hear them. The princess's face softens. "Even when we were children, you wanted me to be only Meryetamun. You wanted to forget what I cannot forget. I am not just Meryetamun. I am also Pharaoh's daughter."

"Which means that you more than anyone cannot disobey his orders!"

Anger returns to her voice. "And have I stopped you from killing babies? No! Have I told you not to kill any-more? No! What order have I disobeyed, Kakemour?" She stops and suddenly tears are in her eyes. "You kill ba-bies and still want me to marry you?"

Kakemour turns a deep red, and when he speaks his words stun me. "Why do you care? They are only Habiru babies. The way these people breed, they will outnumber us before we know it. I do not have the luxury of being able to choose which orders of the pharaoh I will or will not obey. I am only the son of Intef, the *tjat.* The pharaoh orders, I obey."

"My father will not go against what the goddess Taweret has done. My father may even believe, as I do, that the goddess gave me this child as a sign she wants the killing to stop. It is not every day, Kakemour, that the daughter of Pharaoh holds a Habiru baby in her arms. And you saw how the child cried for me when I gave him to his mother. What would your father counsel you to do? Would he tell you to kill the daughter of the pharaoh so you can carry out your orders? And exactly how would you make Ramesses understand why you murdered his favorite daughter? And how do you think he would respond?"

Kakemour looks down, his face twisted in confusion. "All right. We will stop searching for today, and we will escort you back to the palace. As you know, my father, the pharaoh, and your mother, Queen Nefertari, are on their way to Opet for the festival to mark the inundation.

However, Queen Asetnefret, the Second Royal Wife, remains. We will see what she says about all this."

I understand their words but not what they're talking about. Abba looks at me, and I can tell he is anxious to know what has been said. I don't think he is going to like the part about some goddess giving my brother to the princess. What if she is serious? My brother would go to live behind those white walls. But that's where I want to live.

"Come," the princess says to me. "I want to meet your mother."

She follows me into the dark house, through the kitchen and the middle room, and into the front one, where Ima sits on the floor nursing Yekutiel. Aharon and Miryam crouch at her side, looking like the broken wings of a bird. Abba has followed the princess and me into the room and sits down behind Ima.

"You will translate?" the princess asks me.

"I'll try."

The princess kneels on the floor in front of Ima and Abba. Ima looks down at Yekutiel. "I am Princess Meryetamun, daughter of Pharaoh, Lord of the Two Lands, son of the god Amon-Re. Please do not be afraid. I do not mean you or anyone in your family any harm. When I came here some weeks ago, I was upset. Just that morning I had learned from a friend, the soldier I was speaking with outside, that the army would be coming here to kill your newborn sons. I couldn't understand why I was so upset. Like all Khemetians, I had always thought of the

Habiru as uncivilized—with their ugly language, and all that hair your women have on their heads, and the men with hair on their heads and faces. To us a body must be cleaned of hair from head to foot to be attractive and to honor our gods.

"So I was surprised at how distressed I was that a man who wanted to marry me was going to kill babies, even if they were Habiru."

She stops and waits for me to catch up. Ima is looking at her now. Abba's eyes have never left her face.

"I was so upset that I ran from the palace. I didn't have a destination in mind. I needed to get away. I did not know I was in Goshen until I began seeing men and women with their own hair. Then I saw the crocodile kill the baby."

Her voice trembles and she stops. She bites her lip as if trying not to cry. Taking a deep breath, she continues. "Well, I did not actually see it. I saw the crocodile, and I saw the basket and the baby inside. And I saw the crocodile swimming toward the basket. That is when I fainted. If Almah had not been there, it is possible a crocodile might have dragged me into the water."

She turns and looks at me, smiling. "Your daughter is the first person I've ever met who is not afraid of me. I feel like she is more my sister than any of my own. She even dared tell me the truth. People usually tell me only what they think I want to hear.

"If I had wanted to harm you, I would have told the soldiers you were hiding the babies in baskets among the bulrushes on the river. I could have directed them here to your house, where I knew there was a baby. Instead, ever since I was here, I have thought of little else than that baby the crocodile killed. If I had seen the basket sooner, or if I had been more brave, perhaps I could have saved him. But I didn't do anything. Nothing. I didn't even scream. Maybe that would have frightened the crocodile away. I didn't even think to pick up a rock and throw it. I did nothing.

"I was so afraid the soldiers would find your baby. Every morning, when I woke up, the first thing I thought of was Almah and this house and whether your baby was safe. I knew that if I did nothing, the soldiers or a crocodile might eventually find him. This morning I couldn't tolerate it anymore, couldn't tolerate not knowing what had happened to him. So I came to find out.

"The soldiers were just a street away when I got here, and I knew they would be coming to this house soon. I am convinced the goddess led me to the path and the baby. How else could I have found it? When I held him and saw how he looked at me, I knew. He is my son. I want to take him to live with me in the palace and raise him there. Of course, he is still your son, too, but please! I must have this child to raise as my own. Because he is still nursing, would you come and live in the palace and nurse him until he is weaned? And Almah must come to be our translator—and my little sister." The princess looks at me and smiles.

I can't believe what I am hearing. But as I tell Ima, I try to keep any excitement out of my voice. If Ima knows how much I want to go, she will say no. When I finish telling her what the princess has said, I expect Ima to start screaming and yelling. But she doesn't. She looks at the princess. Then she turns and looks over her shoulder at Abba. Yekutiel has finished nursing and lies in the crook of her arm, making little baby sounds and moving his legs. But he is not looking at Ima. He is looking at the princess. I have never seen him this lively. It is as if he has just been born.

The room is so still. Aharon and Miryam look at me, their faces wondering what is wrong. Then Abba asks me in Habiru, "How did she find you and Yekutiel?"

The princess looks at me, expecting me to translate, but I do not. "She said she followed the path through the marsh."

"No!" Ima cuts in. "If a person does not know the path is there, they would not see it. Who led her there?"

"I do not know, Ima. I did not tell her," I add quickly.

"No one is accusing you," Ima says softly.

She is still for a long time. Finally she looks at Abba. If I didn't know him so well, I would not have seen the faint nod of his head. But I do not know what he is saying yes to. I understand only when Ima hands Yekutiel to the princess, tears in her eyes, and says, "My husband said some days ago that Ya, the one god, would use you to stop the killing. In exchange it seems that Ya wants you to have our son."

I do not translate.

"Tell her!" Ima snaps at me.

I do so, afraid the princess is going to start talking about that Taweret goddess. What does it matter if it is

Taweret or Ya who saves my brother? All I care is that Ya and Taweret seem to be in agreement.

"Almah?" It is the princess. "Tell your mother she can bring the two little children. I know it would be hard for them to be separated from her."

I translate, and I am surprised when Ima replies, angrily, "No! I will not give all of my children away. Aharon is with his father all day. A neighbor will take care of Miryam."

Although my wish has come true, I am sorry to be leaving. I will miss watching the sunrise, carrying water from the river, watching Abba pray in the morning, and talking with him before he goes to work. Suddenly I am afraid this is all a mistake, that something is changing forever.

All too soon we are walking to Pi-Ramesses. I wish I could have talked to Abba and heard what he thinks is going to happen, but there was no time. Now there is only silence. I am between the princess—Yekutiel in her arms—and Ima. Abba walks on the other side of Ima. Kakemour is beside the princess, and behind him, the soldiers. On both sides of the road people stand and watch. They, too, are silent.

I try to see us through their eyes. It is not surprising that no one knows what to say. Who has ever seen Pharaoh's daughter walking with Habiru and carrying a Habiru baby? Everyone seems to know that something important is happening, but they do not know what it is. Neither do we who are doing it.

We enter Pi-Ramesses and, after a short distance, turn

up the long walkway of painted stones as smooth as glass that lead to the white walls. However, as we approach the tall doors with the lotus and papyrus painted on them, they swing open. The princess draws in her breath sharply. Standing there is a tall woman wearing a long dress as white and soft as heron feathers. The princess stops. Abba, Ima, and I stop, also. I hear noise behind me and turn to see the soldiers drop to their knees and bow. Kakemour walks past us, however, and only when he is standing directly in front of the woman does he drop to his knees and bend the upper half of his body to the ground. Then he rises and the woman motions him to stand beside her.

"Who is she?" Ima asks me in a whisper.

"I think she is Queen Asetnefret."

She steps out from the shadows into the waning light of the setting sun. Beside me I hear the princess breathing hard, as if she is out of breath from running, though she has been standing still.

"And what do you think you're doing? You would bring a Habiru child into the house of Ramesses?" the queen says in a loud voice.

Ima pinches my arm, wanting to know what she said, but I am afraid to speak.

"Just because you are Ramesses's favorite daughter, it does not mean you can disobey his orders. Do you want me to send word of your impudence to Ramesses?"

"If you wish," the princess responds, her voice almost too soft to be heard.

The queen laughs, but there is no laughter in her

voice or eyes. "Oh, you don't think Ramesses will punish his darling daughter? You are wrong! However, if you give me the child, Ramesses need not hear anything about this."

Ima grabs my arm and shakes it. "What's going on? What did she say?"

I do not answer. Ima looks at Abba. He does not look at her.

"Give me the child!" the queen repeats.

The princess is so still, I wonder if she has died but has not fallen to the ground.

The queen looks at Kakemour and nods. Kakemour begins walking toward us. He is coming to take Yekutiel!

Ima understands now what is about to happen, but before Ima can do anything, the princess says in a strong voice, "You will have to kill me first! And explain that to my father. Even his Second Royal Wife would not be able to convince him it was necessary to kill his favorite daughter. This child is my son, given to me by the goddess Taweret. I do not disobey my father. I obey the goddess."

Kakemour doesn't seem to know whether to keep coming forward, stop where he is, or go back and stand beside the queen. He stops and looks at the queen. I don't know who this Taweret is, but every time the princess mentions her name, it makes a difference.

The queen laughs again. It is a sound you wish you had not heard. "So, this Habiru boy was given to you by Taweret."

"Yes!"

"Then what is his name?"

The queen has obviously said something very important because Kakemour smiles and the soldiers suddenly start talking excitedly among themselves.

"What did she say?" Ima wants to know, concerned.

"The queen asked the princess for Yekutiel's name."

"Then tell the princess. Tell her!"

I turn to the princess and whisper, "His name is—"

"Silence!" she responds harshly, shocking me.

"I'm only trying to help," I insist.

"You aren't."

"What is going on? What is going on?" Ima wants to know.

Before I can say I don't know, I hear the princess announce in a loud voice, "His name is Thutmosis."

Everyone gasps. The queen stares at the princess, and then, without a word, she bows her head and stands to the side. Kakemour does the same and the princess walks forward into the palace, Yekutiel asleep in her arms. Ima and I follow. As I reach the door, I turn around to see Abba. In the darkness he is only a shape among many.

Chapter Six

ONCE A WEEK—every ten days—Abba comes to visit and brings Aharon and Miryam to see Ima. We meet them outside the white walls because he is not allowed inside the Women's Palace. Aharon and Miryam sit with Ima and Mosis, as we call him now, on the grass beneath the shade of a tree. Abba and I sit a distance away, under another tree, where I tell him everything. Well, almost everything.

Abba is glad I'm happy, but I think he's afraid of my being too happy. So I don't tell him that I never want to leave! One of Ima's many stories is about Adam and Chava, the first man and woman. They lived in Gan Eden, a beautiful garden where they never had to work and could have anything they wanted. That is just a story. Living here is real!

"The Women's Palace is so big that when I stand in the hallway outside the princess's suite, I cannot see to the other end. That's where Queen Nefertari lives with her other children, but they're not here now. They're away doing something with the pharaoh. The princess has her own suite because she is an adult now. She has fifteen rooms, each one bigger than our house! The suite is on the second floor. Queen Asetnefret and her children live on the first floor, but they don't talk to us and we don't talk to them."

Abba smiles. "I see."

"I have my own room, Abba."

"A room just for you?"

"A room just for me! It has a balcony, which is like a porch up in the air. Beautiful flowers and plants hang from it, and every day a servant waters them. I sit out there and can see the lake. Can you believe there's a huge lake behind those walls? And from my balcony I can see a pyramid in the distance."

There is so much I want to tell him, and it all tries to come rushing out at once. "And guess what, Abba?" I say, lowering my voice. Without waiting for him to ask "What?" I hurry on before I get too embarrassed. "The bathroom is *inside*! And in the bathroom there's a big smooth stone that slants down, and you lie on it naked and a servant pours water over you and the water goes out through a hole in the floor. The princess says a person must be clean all the time and that body odor is against something called *maat*. The princess takes a bath at least three times a day. And she lets me take baths whenever I want."

"Oh really?" He smiles. "And do you?"

"Three times a day—like her," I say proudly.

I also tell him about my bed! I didn't know such a thing existed. It is four long pieces of wood fastened together to make a square, inside of which are strings that have been plaited together like a mat. Big cushions lie on top of the strings. "And that's what I sleep on. It is so-o-o soft. The first few nights I was afraid I would sink so far down, someone would have to pull me out. Now I don't care if I ever get out."

I expected Abba to chuckle, or at least smile, but he does not respond at all. I'm sorry I said that last part about not ever wanting to get out. "Ima still sleeps on the floor. She says she doesn't want to get used to anything in the house of Pharaoh."

"Your mother is smart."

Now it is my turn not to say anything.

I want to tell him about the princess's huge bed, which has feet that look like a little ugly man. His head is like a lion's, but he is wearing a crown of feathers. He has huge ears, bowed legs, a tail, and he is sticking his tongue out. The princess calls him Bes, the dwarf god, and says he is a friend to women and brings happiness to a house. Even though he's ugly, there's something about him that I like. The princess wanted to give me a necklace with a likeness of him on it, but I didn't take it.

I don't say anything to Abba about all the silence, either. At first it was hard to go to sleep without Abba snoring, Ima grinding her teeth, and the crocodiles roaring. Now I fall asleep and wake up to silence, and I am reluctant to get up because I don't want to wound it.

"I have never seen you like this," Abba remarks. "It is almost as if you have not been happy until now."

It is true, and when I don't deny it, it is as if I nodded.

But I am afraid the princess will send me away in disgust because I am so ignorant. The first meal we had I stood with my mouth open, staring at the gold plates and cups. Until the servants started putting food on the plates and pouring wine into the cups, I didn't know we were going to actually use them. And the food! Every day I can eat antelope, roast duck, roast goose, gazelle, quail, pigeon, or porcupine. There are sweet onions, garlic, leeks, and olives, and the juiciest dates and figs I have ever seen—and something called coconuts, which have milk inside and a white fleshy pulp. They are so good!

Ima says Ya doesn't want us to eat all those things. Maybe Ya isn't as hungry as I am. I didn't know until I moved here, but I think I have been hungry since I was born. I eat so much and it is never enough. When I'm not eating, I'm sleeping, and when I'm not doing either of those, I'm taking a bath or wandering around the palace looking at the walls, which are painted with scenes of marshes and birds flying and fish swimming. It is as if all the beauty of outside has been brought inside, so that when you're inside you can also be outside. I can't believe there are people who can paint animals and trees and fish and make them look real.

My favorite place, though, is the garden, which has trees and grass, baboons, monkeys, and all kinds of birds. In the center is a big lake surrounded by tall palm trees. At the far end is a building with a ramp that extends into the water, a pavilion, the princess called it. Queen Asetnefret likes to sit there in the afternoon with her children.

Ima doesn't like it here, even though the princess has told the servants to treat us as if we are members of her family, to bring us food and drink whenever we want, to walk behind Ima wherever she goes, and to hold a large round fan on a long pole over her head to shade her from the sun—and when she sits down, to fan her from behind. But Ima doesn't want servants doing anything for her. "Ya did not make some people to serve others," she said. "He made us to serve him. I cannot do that if someone is serving me."

I could.

Yet even though she doesn't like it here, she has been asking me to tell her the Khemetian words for things, and the princess has been asking me how to say things in Habiru. I'm afraid if Ima learns Khemetian and the princess learns Habiru, they won't need me anymore and I'll have to return to Goshen. I will kill myself before I go back. I don't say this to Abba, either.

"The soldiers have stayed away," Abba tells me. "You saved our people," he adds.

I shake my head, though I am pleased he thinks so. "I didn't do anything."

"You were not afraid of the princess."

"But I didn't know what that would lead to," I respond.

"No. But Ya did. If you had not gone to the princess when she fainted, Ya would not have been able to do anything. You made it possible for him to use the princess and stop the killing."

I nod as if I understand, but I don't. I'm not even sure I believe in Ya. I'm not sure I ever did. Although I am sad when it is time for Abba to leave, I am also glad. Things are not the same. Aharon and Miryam look at me as if I am a stranger, and when I try to talk to them or play with them, they shrink away from me as if I smell bad. Even Abba looks at me as if he is not sure who I am anymore.

The next day Ima and I are sitting in the garden. We are together now more than ever and I am getting tired of listening to her stories about our ancestors, Avraham and Sarah, Yitzchak and Rivka, and Yaakov and all his wives. I've heard these stories all my life and know them by heart.

"I don't want you to forget where you came from. I don't want you to forget your people," she keeps telling me, her face pinched as if her thoughts hurt her, her shoulders hunched as if she is carrying something heavy inside—too heavy for her thin body.

"I have never seen you so happy," she says.

I am not sure what to say. I am very, very happy but am afraid she will get angry if I say so.

"You and Mosis," she adds, the foreign name said as if there is something bitter on her tongue.

"It is very nice here," I say, keeping pleasure out of my voice.

She is silent again. Then, "Do you believe this Taw-eret gave your brother to the princess?"

Why is she asking me? Is this a trick? If I say yes, I'm in trouble. If I don't say anything, I'm also in trouble. "I . . . I don't know."

There is another long pause. I am afraid to breathe. But when she finally speaks, her voice is softer than I have ever heard it. "It is odd to give birth to a child but never feel the child is yours. Aharon, Miryam—they are my children. I know it without having to think about it. But you and Mosis? When I was carrying you, it was like you were in me but not of me. But you were my first and I thought maybe that's how it is. But with Aharon and Miryam, it was so different. When they were inside me, I talked and sang to them. I never talked or sang to you. Even then it was as if you were someplace I could not reach you. I knew who Aharon and Miryam were by how they moved in my belly. But you kicked and punched me, especially when I tried to sleep. I asked Ya if you were angry. He said no. Mosis was silent. I wondered sometimes if he was dead because he seldom moved. When he was born he did not cry. You seemed to cry only when I came near. I would pick you up and you would kick at me and beat on my arms with your tiny fists. But Amram would just lay his hand on your belly and you would be quiet. When he held you, you did not make a sound. I wondered why you hated me so."

Ima is staring at the lake, but her eyes seem to be looking at something deep in her memory. She has never spoken to me like this, and even though I am sure she is going to say something to hurt me, I don't want her to stop. I wonder if she is waiting for me to apologize for doing things I don't remember, or if she wants me to tell her that I don't hate her. I could tell her that and it would be true. But not all the truth. It is not that I hate her. I don't think I like her—and that's worse, I think.

But before I can figure out what to say, she continues. "You are almost a woman, Almah. Amram doesn't think I understand that. But of course I do. I am a woman. Why wouldn't I understand? But your father loves you more than is good for either of you. Sometimes I think he loves you more than he loves me. He thinks I hate you. You do, too. Don't you?"

She looks at me for the first time. I want to lie, but I blush and she can see the truth.

She opens her arms. Hesitantly I move closer, and she puts her arms around me and holds me tightly. I am trying hard not to cry.

"I am sorry, my daughter. I do not hate you. I love you. You are my firstborn and therefore you will always be special. But I am frightened. You are my daughter, my firstborn, and yet I do not know you. You have never needed me except when I nursed you. A mother likes to feel needed, likes to feel that her children will come to her with questions and problems. You never have. You've always gone to your father. You need him. You even need the princess. I see you look at her as you have never looked at me. And now there is Mosis, who cries when I pick him up and smiles when the princess holds him. I have a son and cannot call him by the name I gave him. That night I did not know. If I had known that the princess was giving him a name, and her doing so gave her power over him, that she was naming him for an idol that has the head of an ibis, I think I would have died before I let her do it."

"But he is named for the god of wisdom," I protest, "the god who loves truth."

Ima looks at me with disgust. "There is no god but Ya!" Then she sighs. "Often I have wondered why he gave you and Mosis to me. I've asked him if he didn't make a mistake. And now, when I see how happy you are here among idolaters, when I see how happy Mosis is with the princess, I am glad I believe in Ya as deeply as I do. Otherwise I would think your true mother was this Taweret."

She starts crying, then gets up and hurries into the palace. I want to run after her and tell her there was no mistake. Just because you're born to someone, it doesn't mean you belong to them.

THE NEXT MORNING Ima has just finished nursing Mosis. As she hands him to the princess, she says, "I gave birth to him, but Ya wants him to be your son."

I look at her sharply, my face asking if she really wants me to translate that. And I don't understand. Yesterday she was saying Taweret gave us to the princess.

"Tell her," Ima orders me.

I do. The princess looks at Ima, a quizzical expression on her face. "How do you know?"

"I prayed to Ya most of the night. I am not happy that my son and my daughter are happier in the palace of an idolater than with their mother. But Ya told me that this is what he wants. I do not understand. But just as our father, Avraham, obeyed when Ya told him to sacrifice his favorite son, I will obey now."

"Who is this Ya you're always talking about, Yocheved?" the princess asks. "What does he look like?"

"He cannot be seen," Ima says.

"Then how do you know he exists or where he is? There are statues of Ramesses all over Khemet so that wherever the people are, they can see their god."

"Statues can break," Ima responds, a sly smile on her lips. "The invisible god is everywhere at the same time and is eternal. It was Ya who sent you to Goshen."

The princess laughs lightly. "That's ridiculous."

"Is it? Think about it. You had never been there in your life. Yet you just happen into Goshen on the day and at the exact time a crocodile killed a baby someone had hidden on the river. You fainted exactly when Almah happened to be watching. Any other Habiru girl would have left you there. My people do not think too highly of Khemetians. But you just happened to faint in front of the one Habiru girl who speaks your language fluently. I say all this was the work of Ya."

"It *is* odd," the princess admits reluctantly. "But why can't you believe in this Ya of yours and our gods, too?"

"Your country is great and powerful, isn't it?"

"Yes, it is."

"Many peoples pay tribute to Pharaoh and bow to him as a god."

"Yes."

"Except the Habiru. We are the only ones who do not

bow to Pharaoh. If we were not sure that Ya exists and is greater than Pharaoh, we would have bowed our heads to your father many, many years ago. Your father is merely a man who will one day die. Like me. Like you. How can someone be a god if his end is the same as mine?"

"I never thought of that," the princess responds, as if what Ima said made sense. I want to tell her that a god who cannot die does not know what it is like to be a person, cannot understand us. Why is the princess looking at Ima as if she is wonderful?

Chapter Seven

"RAMESSES IS RETURNING!"

Queen Asetnefret's loud voice in the main room of the suite wakes me. Ima comes in from her room next door, her eyes asking me what is going on. Whispering, I translate.

"But why?" the princess responds. "The Festival of Opet has scarcely begun."

Asetnefret laughs that laugh that makes me think about preparing to die. "I sent word to him that you are out of control and disobeying his orders. It seems he is sufficiently distressed that he is coming back immediately. If I were you I'd get this Habiru woman, her daughter, and that baby out of here today. If they aren't here, especially the baby, Ramesses might forgive you. Let me put it this way. I can guarantee you that Ramesses will forgive you."

"What're you talking about?" The princess's voice is angry. "You talk like Ramesses does whatever you say."

"You are naive, Meryetamun. Just because your mother, Nefertari, is always at Pharaoh's side, it does not mean she has influence. Ramesses likes beautiful women, and even I will admit that your mother is the most beautiful woman I have ever seen. If I were Pharaoh, I would want a thing of beauty by my side, too. However, when he needs to talk about important matters, he talks to me. It was I who persuaded him that the Habiru were becoming too numerous and could not be trusted. Ramesses is too busy bringing new wives into his harem and fathering children to know when his reign is threatened."

"I *knew* it! I knew my father would not have thought of something like that. I knew it!"

Queen Asetnefret says something else, but I can't hear it, and then it is silent, except for the sound of the princess crying softly. The queen must have left. Ima and I walk quietly along the corridor and into the main room. The princess sits on a couch, her legs tucked beneath her, her head down. Ima sits down next to her and puts her arms around her as she has never put them around me. I do not want to look. Then I think, maybe the princess's mother will love me like my mother loves the princess.

I go into the room next to the princess's bedroom, the one where she keeps the jars of colors she puts on her eyes and lips and cheeks. I sit down on the stool before a low table where the jars are arranged neatly in a row. On the table also is a mirror whose handle is in the shape of the naked body of a woman with long, beautiful legs. Her arms curve over her head to form a circle, inside of which is a disk of pure gold that shines like the sun. But her arms are not just arms. They are also wings with long feathers, each one carved from gold. (*"Her name is Eset, but we also call her Mut-netjer, the Mother of the Gods. Khemetians love her more than they do any other goddess. She is selfless. She has great powers, but she uses them for others. Every morning, when I hold this mirror, it is like reminding myself to be like her. I suppose it was Eset who led me to return to Goshen and try to save your brother.")*

I should not be in here by myself, though the princess has never said I couldn't. Every morning I sit on the floor and watch as the two servants put the colors on her face and rub the sweet-smelling oils into her body. More than once she has asked me if I want color around my eyes, or maybe a tiny bit of red on my lips. I shake my head, but my heart is pounding—*yes, yes, yes!*

I look at the mirror and Eset almost seems alive. I know the mirror was made by someone, that Eset is not really alive, but looking at her makes me hope that when I am a woman, my breasts will be proud and full like hers. How could someone make something so beautiful—and from gold—if it were not alive somewhere? I do not know if Eset really exists, but the feelings I have when looking at her are real. This is how I wanted to feel those mornings when I stood naked by the river and faced the sun. Maybe that's what Eset and Taweret and all the other gods and goddesses do. They help us see our feelings. They help us see who we are and who we can be.

I touch her foot lightly. The gold is cool and hard. I let my fingers go slowly and lightly up and down the legs, and then to the round breasts, the arms, and along the feathers. Over and over my fingers caress her. Maybe if I touch her long enough, I, too, will be able to stand naked and beautiful, and then my arms will become wings.

I don't mean to, but my hand curls around the handle and I raise the mirror and am startled by the face I see. The girl looking back at me has long, curly dark hair. Her eyes are dark, also, and shaped like narrow almonds. The nose is also narrow, but it is her lips that stand out. It is as though her face decided to wait and find all its expression in lips that are large and full. I do not know what to think. It is different looking at myself here than seeing my reflection in the river. I think I may be beautiful. Or I could be.

I take the lids from the jars and look at the colors inside. They are shiny and oily. The princess puts red on her cheeks, but what would it be like to wear the sky on your face and to put the color of blood around your eyes? (*"Wearing paint around the eyes protects them from the sun as well as makes one look more beautiful."*) I am afraid I will get paint in my eyes, but what if I put a little red on my lips? Just a little. Not enough even that anyone would notice.

I put my little finger lightly into the red paint and touch it to my bottom lip and rub it in all the way across. I hold up the mirror. My lip looks as if it is on fire! I put a little more paint on my finger and rub it across my top lip. I look in the mirror again. My lips look like the sunset. I take more paint and rub it into my cheeks. My face looks like a flower!

I take off my dress and stand stiffly, my legs together, and raise my arms above my head in a circle. I wish I could see myself, wish I could see if I look like Eset. I think I do because I don't feel like Almah anymore, and maybe that is why I do not hear the door open.

"What are you doing?"

I drop my arms immediately, hurriedly pick my dress up from the floor and slip it over my head. "Just . . . just pretending," I say to Ima, my voice barely audible.

"You look beautiful," the princess says. She is smiling. "I knew you would."

I want to smile back, but Ima's eyes are holding me as if she has her hands around my throat. "You look like a Khemetian whore!" she spits at me. "What do you think your father would say if he saw you like this?"

I cannot look at her and my eyes drop to the floor. But then I remember Eset. I remember the feeling she gave me and I don't want to lose it. I force myself to look up. Ima's face is angry. It hurts to be looked at with anger.

"Wipe that paint off your face. I am sending you back to Goshen!"

I don't know what to do. I look at the princess. Her face is like a question mark. I translate what Ima said, then add, "I think I'll die if I have to go back there."

"Then stay," the princess responds simply. "It would be good for your brother to grow up knowing his oldest sister."

"What did she say?" Ima asks angrily.

I hesitate.

"What did you say to her and what did she say?" Ima asks again, more angry now.

"She said she will need help raising Mosis and it would be better for him if it came from his own sister rather than one of the servants."

I have never lied to Ima. I have never needed to. Until

now. Ima is looking me directly in the eye. I stare back at her. If she would let me be myself, I wouldn't have to lie.

It is Ima whose eyes waver first. She looks away, then down toward the floor. Quickly she raises her head and stares at me, but I do not blink or look away. I stare back at her as if my eyes are suns. She blinks and her eyes waver again, then shift to the side. I can't believe it! I have won! Ima will never be able to hurt me again!

Chapter Eight

THE PHARAOH HAS RETURNED! The princess and Queen Asetnefret went to the big palace yesterday, and neither has come back. A high wall with a gate separates the Women's Palace from the palace where the pharaoh lives. I went to the gate, but the guards stopped me, wanting to know who I was and what I wanted and what was a Habiru doing there?

With the princess gone, I have no one to talk to. Ima has not spoken to me since that morning. I sit in the garden hoping to see the princess returning. Why has she been gone so long? She is pleading with Pharaoh not to send us back to Goshen. Will I be sitting here in the garden next month, feeling the warmth of the sun on my skin, watching the baboons in the trees and the geese on the lake? Or will I be dead? Those are the only choices.

Will Abba understand if I never return to Goshen? Will he understand why I need a goddess, why I need to be able to see that goddess and touch her? How can I make him understand when I do not?

"Almah?"

The sound of someone calling my name startles me. I look around. It is Kakemour! I quickly get to my feet. There is so much about Khemetian ways I do not know. Do you bow to a soldier? Am I supposed to call him by a special title?

"Oh, you don't have to get up," he says kindly. "May I sit down?"

I hesitate. Why is he here? Has he come to send me back to Goshen? Is he going to kill Mosis this time? But he is being nice to me. Why?

"I can understand that you might not want to sit with me. I . . . I was not exactly friendly the last time we saw each other. If you let me sit down, perhaps I can explain. Or at least apologize."

Slowly I sit back down and motion him to sit down also. He looks so different without a spear in his hand, without all the soldiers around, without Queen Asetnefret giving orders. I hope I am not being rude, but I look at his face and I like that I can see his skin and how smooth it is. I can even see the line of his jaw, and it is strong. Abba says Ya wants the Habiru to cover their faces with hair. Why would Ya care about hair? Suddenly I am aware that I have never been so close to a man so young and handsome. He smells like flowers and his skin glistens like the sun on the river. I want to put my hand on his chest.

"I don't know what happened to me that day," he says softly. "Before we went I thought I was going to enjoy it. Meryetamun and I sat right here on this bench a few weeks before, and I told her the pharaoh had ordered us to kill all the newborn male children in Goshen. I didn't think she would care. But she was furious. She ran away and ended up in Goshen, where you found her.

"It was my first assignment as a soldier. I wanted to do well and make my father proud of me. Make the pharaoh proud of me. I said some ugly and hateful things about your people and I'm sorry. I hope you will forgive me. I did not want the other soldiers to think I was weak. But I hated what we did there. I hope you believe me when I say that I did not kill any babies. Please tell the princess that for me."

"But you didn't stop anyone else from killing them," I say flatly. "And what would you have done if Queen Asetnefret had told you to kill my brother?"

His head drops. "I . . . I don't know. I think I probably would have obeyed. I could not have gone against *maat*. I'm sorry."

"I am, too," I say quietly.

"At least you will tell the princess for me that I did not kill any babies. She's going to need a friend now."

"What do you mean?"

"You don't know?"

"Know what?"

"Her mother, Queen Nefertari, died suddenly in Opet. That is why the pharaoh has returned."

"Oh no!" I exclaim. "I am so sorry."

"So am I. She was a wonderful woman. I don't think any woman has ever been loved as much as the pharaoh loved her. My father says he is not sure if the pharaoh himself will survive the shock of not having Queen Nefertari beside him every day. They were inseparable."

"Your father is *tjat*?"

"Yes. And I will become *tjat* when he dies."

"Yosef was *tjat*," I put in.

"Who?"

"Yosef. My mother tells stories about Yosef. He was one of our ancestors who became the second most powerful man in Khemet."

"Psontenpa'anh."

"Who?"

"That is the name of your Yosef in Khemetian. You should be careful not to tell your mother's stories to a Khemetian."

"Why? Maybe if people knew the story of Yosef they would be nicer to the Habiru."

"Maybe if you knew the true story you would understand why we do not like Habiru."

"What do you mean?" I ask, curious and afraid.

"Many years ago a people called the Amu lived among us. Over time their numbers increased until there were almost as many of them as us, and they gained power. Their leader called himself Pharaoh, but he was a false pharaoh who destroyed our temples and enslaved our people. Your Yosef was *tjat* to this pharaoh. Your Yosef helped him enslave our people by making them sell their bodies into slavery in exchange for grain during a long famine. That is why now, when the pharaoh saw that there were more and more Habiru, he became afraid that they would take over again as they did when they joined with the Amu."

"But we do not want to rule your country. We only want to be allowed to go to the land Ya promised us."

Kakemour nods. "I know. But we remember what happened before."

I am angry. "Well, I don't believe your story. It's not true!"

"Well, it is as true for us as your story is for you. It is what we believe, and that is why we do not trust Habiru." Kakemour gets up. "I have to go. Please tell Meryetamun that if she needs a friend now, I am here."

I nod. As I watch him walk quickly away, I wish there were someone I could talk to. How can two stories be true? Or is something true only because a lot of people believe it?

Chapter Nine

I AM SORRY I NEVER MET Queen Nefertari. She must have been a wonderful mother, because the princess has done almost nothing but cry for a week now. She wails and screams and sobs until she is exhausted. Then she sleeps for a little while, only to awake and begin crying again. Ima is with her almost all the time, holding her, talking to her, singing to her. They do not ask me to translate and I do not want to.

Sadness fills the palace like the waters of the river that have spread over the land. Everyone walks slowly and speaks softly. Many have tears in their eyes, especially the servants. People tell me how beautiful and kind and wonderful she was, as if by speaking of her they can bring her back to life. By the way they have been talking to me about her, I think people are getting used to me and are seeing me as one of them. Maybe that is because I paint my cheeks and lips every morning, but not my eyes—yet.

I am sitting in the garden and suddenly everything is still. The servants working by the lake are looking toward the long pathway leading to the gate between this palace and the big one. Suddenly everyone drops to their knees and their bodies bend over until their heads touch the ground.

I turn to see what is happening, and when I see him come through the gate, I slip from the bench and drop to my knees, also. I do not intend to. It just happens. I have never seen him, but I know who it is! I should bow, but I don't want to because I have never seen a god.

The pharaoh is tall and wears a headdress colored blue like early morning. From the center of it extends the head of a cobra. The bottom is covered by a broad band of gold. His face is long and narrow, and the line of his jaw looks as strong as an arm. His eyes are set deep back in his head like a hawk's. He is wearing a long white robe and beneath it a garment of yellow. Around his neck is a large necklace of blue, red, and yellow jewels.

He must be going to see the princess. No. He is turning up the stone walk that leads this way! I know I should bow or run or do something, but I cannot move and I cannot take my eyes off him. Only when he looks directly into my eyes does my body let go, and my head touches the ground.

"You must be Almah." I hear a soft and low voice.

I raise my head but do not get to my feet. I do not know what to say. He did not ask me if I was Almah. He knew. Why would the pharaoh know who I am?

He stares at me with small, piercing dark eyes. Then he smiles. It is a sad smile, but a smile, nonetheless. "I understand now," he says, looking over his shoulder at the two men standing a short distance behind him. It is

Kakemour, and next to him, a small man who must be the *tjat*, Kakemour's father. For some reason Kakemour is smiling at me.

"You will sit with me?" the pharaoh says.

I am speechless. The pharaoh wants me to sit with him? As I get to my feet I wonder if he has come in person to send me back to Goshen because the princess would not do it. But if he were going to send me away, he would not have smiled at me.

The pharaoh sits on the bench and beckons me to sit beside him. Two tall male servants arrange themselves behind him, and with their long-handled feathered fans, create a gentle breeze. "Come," he says to me.

I get up and sit timidly at the edge of the bench. Kakemour stands beside me while his father stands on the other side, next to the pharaoh. I dare to look at Pharaoh. He does not look like a god. Just a very sad man. His eyes are red and puffy like the princess's, and his body sags into itself as if he is too weary to hold it up.

"I am sorry about the death of the queen," I offer quietly.

He looks at me, but I cannot tell if I should have said that. His gaze returns to the lake. "This was *her* favorite place to sit," he says.

"Oh. I didn't know." Is he offended to find me sitting where his dead wife sat? "It . . . it is very peaceful here," I add, seeking to explain.

"Do you sit here often?"

"Yes, I do."

"And what do you think about when you sit here?"

No one except Abba has ever asked me what I think. Maybe people like Abba and the pharaoh ask you what you think because they really want to know. So I tell him, "That I hope I never have to live in Goshen again." I feel his eyes on me, but I do not look up. I do not want to see what he might be thinking.

"You like it here?"

"I love it here!"

"And why is that?"

"Because everything is perfect," I tell him.

"But isn't everything perfect in Goshen?"

I am silent as I think about his question. Finally I say, "I don't know. I never thought about anything being perfect until the princess brought me here."

"But don't you believe in a god who is greater than Pharaoh? Doesn't this Ya make life perfect for you?" His voice is sharp, almost angry.

"I don't know much about Ya," I reply simply, which is true, and I don't want to talk about any of that. I want to know about the pharaoh.

He frowns. "Is something wrong?" he asks.

"No. Why do you ask?"

"You are staring at me as if my nose is on crooked or something."

I blush. "I am sorry. Please accept my apology. I was wondering about the snake on your headdress."

He chuckles and looks at Kakemour's father, who returns a weak smile. I don't know what is so funny. He turns back to me and explains. "That is the goddess Wadjet.

She protects Khemet. She also protected the goddess Eset and her newborn son, Hor, from the evil god Sutekh."

"Eset is beautiful!" I exclaim.

"Oh? And what do you know about Eset?"

"Nothing, except the princess has a beautiful mirror."

"Ah yes!" Then he is quiet. "That was Nefertari's mirror. I gave it to her some years ago and she gave it to Meryetamun."

"I did not know," I say apologetically.

"Did not know what?"

"That it was a gift from Queen Nefertari. I would not have used it had I known."

"You did no harm. What was it like to use it, Almah?"

"Oh, I have never held anything so beautiful in my life! I liked how heavy it felt in my hand and how it seemed to shine as if something were glowing inside. I liked how beautiful the goddess was, how proud and how strong she was even though she did not have on any clothes. And I liked seeing what I look like. I had only seen my face in the river, but looking at myself in the mirror—" I stop, embarrassed by what I was about to say.

"Go on."

I shake my head. "No. That's all right."

"I take it that you liked seeing yourself," the pharaoh says, as if he understands.

I nod. "Yes. Yes, I did. I had never known what I really look like."

"And what did you think?"

I am blushing. "That maybe I am pretty." I look up at

the pharaoh, hoping to see that sad smile. Instead tears are coming down his face.

"What's the matter?" I ask. "Did I say something wrong?"

He does not say anything for a long time. Finally he says, "You remind me so much of her. She was your age when I married her. I sit here with you, and you are so honest and open and inquisitive and full of life, and yes, beautiful. It is as if her *ka*—her spirit—is alive in you."

"I . . . I don't understand."

"You have the same heart as the queen," Kakemour puts in. "I noticed it when we spoke here a few days ago. The queen was not afraid, just as you are not."

That is what Ima said to Abba about me. "She is not afraid." Ima didn't like that. The pharaoh does.

Kakemour continues. "The other day when I saw you sitting here on the bench, it reminded me of all the times I saw the queen sitting here, and you looked just like her in how you seemed to want to take everything into yourself—the sun, the water, the birds, the air. I told my father and he told the pharaoh and the pharaoh wanted to see you for himself."

The pharaoh touches my arm lightly and then gets up and walks back toward the big palace. Queen Asetnefret has come out of the Women's Palace and moves toward him as if to speak, but he does not look in her direction. It is as if she does not exist to him.

"You made the pharaoh smile and laugh for the first time since the queen died," Kakemour whispers in my ear before he hurries to follow his father and the pharaoh. Only after they disappear from my view do I realize that everyone is staring at me, especially Asetnefret.

The next morning, I am eating breakfast when the princess comes to my room. "Someone is here to see you." Her voice sounds strained, and there is a look of both surprise and unhappiness on her face.

I go into the main room, where Ima and the princess are, and I am surprised to see Kakemour. Behind him are four servants. Two hold oblong golden boxes. The other two hold large baskets.

"Welcome in peace!" I greet him.

"In peace. In peace," he returns, smiling. "The pharaoh would be honored if you would accept these gifts."

I do not understand. A servant steps forward and, bowing, opens the box and places it at my feet. It is filled with bracelets, anklets, rings, earrings, and necklaces made of gold and jewels of reds and greens and blues. I cannot help but gasp at their beauty. But almost immediately another servant places her box beside the first one and opens it. More jewelry! I have never seen so many jewels in one place. The next servant places a basket on the floor and opens it. Inside are folded dresses of the purest white linen. The last servant opens her basket and reveals jars of ointments and colors and a mirror almost identical to the one the princess has. However, this one is more beautiful. The goddess has diamonds for eyes and a ruby for lips, and her golden feathers are embedded with jewels. As I hold it up, I hear a gasp from the princess.

I do not know what to say or do. I cannot believe all this is for me! Ima will never let me keep any of it. But then Kakemour says, "The pharaoh would also be honored if you would accept these two as your personal servants." He points to the ones who had carried the golden boxes. "Finally, the pharaoh would like you to have your own suite, a small suite, which is part of what was Queen Nefertari's large suite. The pharaoh would be honored to know that someone is living in part of the space that was hers."

I feel as if I am going to faint. My own suite! My own servants! The pharaoh wants me to live here for . . . for . . . forever, it seems. I will never have to go back to Goshen. I know I should say something, should express my thanks, but I could never put all I am feeling into words. Still, I must try.

"Please tell the son of Amon-Re, the Lord of the Two Lands, he whose prayers cause the sun to rise, that I am unworthy of such attention. I accept these gifts as expressions of his great generosity and hope that one day I will merit them."

Kakemour is impressed and so am I. "I will have your gifts taken to your rooms. You may occupy them anytime you are ready."

Kakemour and the four servants are scarcely out the door before Ima screams at me, "What did you do? No man gives a woman all that for nothing!"

"Ima!" I exclaim. "I have done nothing."

"Not yet! No man gives a woman gold and jewels without wanting something in return!"

I know what she is thinking. I know what she wants to call me, and I dare her to say it! I dare her!

"Tell her my father is not like that," the princess interjects. Although Ima and I spoke in Habiru, she understood Ima's tone of voice and angry eyes. "He is very generous to those who touch his heart."

I am surprised to hear the princess's voice break with bewilderment, hurt, and anger as she asks, "What did you do? I didn't know you knew my father. When did this happen?"

I tell her about yesterday, and as I translate for Ima, the princess starts crying softly. When I am done, the princess says wistfully, "When I was little I would sit on my mother's lap while the servants put on her makeup. She had two mirrors. She would never let me touch the one with the jewels in it, but she said that one day it would be mine. Maybe Father didn't know. Maybe he didn't care. I am not sure. But the mirror he gave to you is the one my mother said she was going to give to me."

"You can have it," I say immediately, meaning it. "I didn't know. I would feel better if you had it. I'm sure he didn't know your mother promised it to you."

The princess shakes her head. "I didn't see it before now. How could I have not? Probably because of your hair. But if I imagine you wearing a wig, it is obvious. You look like my mother did when I was a girl." She shakes her head again. "And I brought you here!" She stops. "I'm sorry, Almah. None of this is your fault. You are just being yourself. Who can fault you for that? And I can't blame Father, either. Thank you for offering me the mirror, but it is not that simple. You cannot refuse a gift from the pharaoh. Especially that gift. Don't you understand what his giving you my mother's mirror means?" she asks, hurt and anger coming back into her voice.

I don't know what she is talking about. I translate for Ima, and when I finish there is a long silence. Finally Ima looks at me and says, her voice filled with contempt, "You are now Pharaoh's daughter!"

Part Two

YEAR 29 OF THE REIGN OF RAMESSES THE GREAT,
4TH MONTH OF SHEMU, DAY 12

Chapter One

"MOSIS, YOU'RE THE ONLY man I know who has three mothers," Kakemour teases me.

It is evening and we are walking on the other side of the river. This is where Kakemour taught me to drive a chariot. The earth is sandy here like the desert. Looking back across the river, I can still see myself the first time I held the reins as we came out of the stable, through the gates, and over the dike to this place where the earth moves like water.

That seems so long ago. I had nothing to worry about then. Now I am old enough to marry but I am not interested in women. Kakemour takes me to dinners at the homes of noblemen with beautiful daughters eager to marry the pharaoh's grandson, or to taverns on the side streets off the Avenue of the Crocodiles in the Workers' Village. If we keep walking in this direction we'll end up in one of those places, or worse. Kakemour worries about me and I do, too. I have no interest in women. I am old enough to have an occupation, but there is nothing I want to do. I do not understand what is wrong with me.

I don't know what to say. No. That is not true. There are some things I could say but something stops me from talking to him about the ones he calls my "three mothers." I think he knows and is a little angry. That is why he is teasing me.

"Why would any man need *three* of them?" he continues, chuckling quietly. "Please understand. I love my mother, but one is enough!"

Later that evening, when I am alone again in my suite, I, too, wonder why three women have raised me, three women who are so different and yet agree about their love for me.

Ima says I am special to Ya. I wish I knew why, and what he wants me to do. Mother tells me to be patient. But I am tired of waiting and tired of not knowing what I am waiting for. And how do I even know if I am waiting for anything? This could be how things are meant to be. I will always be the Habiru who is not really Habiru, the Khemetian who is not really Khemetian, the grandson of the pharaoh who is not really his grandson. I will always be pretending to be something I'm not and never knowing who I really am.

Almah says I have trouble talking because I don't know yet which "me" should be using my voice. She is partially right. In my dreams I speak Habiru and Khemetian, sometimes both in the same sentence. But there's another reason, one I have not told anyone, not even her. I am afraid to say what I really feel because I am not always sure if those feelings are mine or someone else's. I can feel what others feel, even when they are trying to hide their feelings or hide from them.

Mother and Almah have each told me about the first months of my life, when the army was looking for Habiru male babies. I do not remember that, of course. But I still remember the silence of Abba and Ima was as powerful as the jaws of a crocodile. Their fear was as cold and deep as the Great Green Sea, and it closed my throat so tightly that I could not cry, even when I was hungry.

Almah said I never made a happy sound until Mother held me the first time. I remember the smell of sun and wind on soft warm skin and the feeling that I was safe at last. Most of all I remember listening to Mother's heart singing. I did not know that is what hearts are supposed to do, until she pressed me against hers.

Ima never talked of those times. She spoke only about Ya and our ancestors. I have never been able to know her feelings. It is as if she is made of stone and her feelings are buried deep like the mummies of the pharaohs of ancient times that are hidden in the secret chambers of the pyramids. I know her feelings are there, but I do not know what they are. Maybe all her feelings belong to Ya, because she has never talked of much else to me.

"Why you speak so much of Ya?" I asked her once.

She frowned. I knew it was not my question that bothered her but the way I spoke. It has always bothered her. When I was still a child she told me, "You talk like you are ignorant. You don't have to talk like that. Why do you?"

I did not know how to explain to her that words feel like stones in my mouth. I do not like words and do not trust them. I know I sound sometimes like I am not very intelligent. In my mind words flow like the Hapi. But when they reach my tongue, they start to go backward, as if they do not want to leave me, as if they do not want anyone to hear them except me. It is hard to talk about that to someone as sure of her opinions as Ima. So I said nothing that day. I have never said much when I'm with her, which is not often these days.

"I did not talk about Ya enough to your sister, and look what happened," she said finally, in answer to my question. "She forgot who she was. She betrayed us and she betrayed Ya."

But Almah did not forget and she betrayed no one. She simply does not believe. I wonder if Ima would understand if she saw Almah dance at a festival. Grandfather says Almah causes the goddesses to walk among the people. Ima could not see that because she does not believe in goddesses. That is why she and Almah cannot talk to each other. Neither believes what the other believes.

It is Shemu, Harvest Season. The river is at its lowest, and almost everyone in Khemet works in the fields, harvesting the grain and vegetables, even those like Abba and Aharon who ordinarily work building the temples.

When the harvest is done, I will start going outside the palace grounds again during the day. It never bothered me, until this year. Now I am terrified that if I go outside I will see Aharon, Abba, Ima, and Miryam sweating in the fields. I am terrified they will look up and see me and hate me. I am afraid all of the Habiru will see me and hate me. But they probably do already.

I am Habiru. I should be out there with them. But I don't want to be. I am glad I don't have to work in the hot sun all day getting my hands dirty, and my body becoming smelly and slick with sweat. And I hate myself for feeling like this. But I am glad I am not a slave.

I wish I could talk to someone. Kakemour would not understand. Almah understands me better than anybody, but she is a priestess. She knows who she is. I feel as if I will never know who I am.

If I could be anybody in Khemet, I wish I could be Almah. I don't think even Grandfather is as happy to be who he is as Almah is to be a priestess and dance naked at the temple.

"Why don't you believe in Ya?" I asked her once.

"Ya does not make me want to dance. When I dance, the people see that Hathor and Eset are real. When I think about Ya, I do not feel like dancing. This is what I was born to do, Mosis."

"What was I born to do, Almah?"

She hugged me to her. "I don't know. You will find out one day."

I was ten the first time I saw her dance. It was during the festival of Hathor, protector of women and the goddess of dance, love, and joy. We were outside the Great Temple in Pi-Ramesses. Its columns are so tall that even now I have to bend my head all the way back to see to the top. Unlike other temples, whose outside walls are carved with scenes of Grandfather standing in his chariot, pulling a bow and arrow, and leading the charge against the Hittites at the Battle of Kadesh, the outside of the Great Temple is white and a large cow with stars in her belly—the goddess Hathor—is painted on it. Abba was one of the workmen who put the huge stones in place, and my brother, Aharon, helped paint the picture of the goddess.

I sat between Grandfather and Mother at the entrance to the temple, statues of a seated pharaoh on either side of us. From where we sat we could see all four sections of the city and their temples, each dedicated to a god or goddess—Wadjet ruled the northern section, Seth the south, Astarte the east, and Amon the west. The temples are taller than the other buildings, and because of their colorful walls of green, red, blue, and white and the pictures of the gods or goddesses painted on them—regardless of where you are in the city—you have only to raise your eyes and you will be reminded of *maat* and that your life and everything you do helps create divine order.

I liked sitting above the people, liked that they were looking up and pointing excitedly at Ramesses, and I imagined them wondering who the boy was sitting next to him. I was on his right and Mother was next to me. Intef and Kakemour sat on the other side, where Queen Nefertari would have sat if she had been alive. Almah told me that there had been another queen, Asetnefret, but no one seemed to know where she was or what had happened to her.

Below us was the temple porch, where the dancing would be. Below the porch, at the bottom of the broad steps leading up to it, the mass of people extended as far as I could see along the Avenue of Hathor, which led to the temple. Round columns, sixty feet high, bordered both sides of the street. Images of the gods and goddesses had been cut into each one, and from where I sat, the carvings looked like the shadows of leaves flickering against tree bark. Beneath the columns the people were smaller and less consequential than half-completed thoughts. On the first, sixth, seventh, fifteenth, and twenty-third of each month, there was a festival. No one worked on those days, and people could eat and drink as much as they wanted, the meat and beer a gift of the pharaoh.

At the first jingling sound of the *shesheset*, everyone quieted. The person shaking it could not be seen, but the sound signaled that the dancing was about to begin. The *shesheset* is a long-handled instrument holding an oblong frame, inside of which are metal disks threaded onto small rods. A soft musical sound is made when it is shaken. I had seen Almah's *shesheset* many times in her suite. It was made especially for her because she is the priestess of Hathor. There is only one like it. Larger than the ordinary ones, it is of fine gold, so that it constantly flashes, sending light back to the sun even as it receives light. The head of Hathor is carved on each side of the handle, while the frame is shaped like the curved horns of a bull. Hathor was the mother of Amon-Re, the sun god, and she held the sun between her horns, and stars in her belly.

Even though I could not see who was shaking the *shesheset,* I knew from the sound it was Almah. The rhythm she was making with it filled me with a tension that became tighter and tighter until, just as I was ready to scream or shout or do something that would have been out of character, suddenly, from the right side of the porch, my sister leaped out, naked, the *shesheset* in her hand, the light from its gold flashing across our eyes in the rhythm of its beat.

Both Grandfather and Mother had told me Almah would be dancing that day, and I knew that the priestesses danced naked. People in Khemet do not wear many clothes, anyway. But this was my sister! I did not want her showing her body to everyone. I did not want all those eyes fixed on her as if she were a roasted bullock they were about to eat. Most of all, I did not want to look at her, even though I could not turn my eyes away.

But now the porch was filled with the sound of drums, and the music of flutes and horns as the musicians, all naked women, danced out from the opposite side and seated themselves at the back.

As I watched Almah leap and spin and somersault across the porch, something odd happened. I stopped seeing her as my sister, and she became someone who merely *looked* like my sister. I was enthralled by her beauty, her joy, her lack of self-consciousness, and no longer cared who she was. I cared only that she never stopped leaping and spinning to the beat of the drums, the *shesheset,* and the music of the flutes and horns.

My eyes widened and my heart beat faster as the

rhythms pounded at me like the heartbeat of the sun. I felt like I, too, wanted to dance, could dance—and more, *should*. The crowd below started clapping their hands in rhythm to the drums. I closed my eyes, and my body began swaying from side to side. Nothing existed anymore except the melodies and rhythms filling the air, and I thought I could feel the passion throbbing in the hearts of everyone in the crowd, and I, too, wanted to be naked and beautiful and to dance for the goddess, and I started to get up from my seat as my hands dropped to my hips to take off my kilt.

Suddenly Ima's face came into my mind like a funeral mask, and just like that, all the passion, joy, and love for the goddess that had been rising through my body like the sun reaching for midday were drowned in a sadness as bottomless as night. My body stopped moving and I stood still as if I had been turned into a statue. Then I slumped slowly into my seat, alone and empty.

I was a mere spectator now, watching a beautiful woman spinning in time to the music, which became faster—but no matter how fast the musicians played, she spun faster and leaped higher.

I happened to glance at Grandfather. His eyes had grown large and were fixed on Almah, and his mouth was open, his lips glistening with moisture. I was too young then to know the word *lust*, but I felt in him a yearning as broad and wide and deep as the Hapi when it has reached its height, a desire more intense than the sun on the sand and a hunger nothing could satisfy.

The music and drums played even faster and Almah

did a series of back flips and just as she disappeared from view, the music and rhythm stopped abruptly. All the people erupted into shouting and cheering and then they started chanting, "Meryetamun! Meryetamun! Meryetamun!"

I did not understand. "Why chant for you?" I asked Mother.

"That is your sister's Khemetian name," she said in a tight voice. After a pause, she continued in a voice that tried to sound cordial but was as empty of warmth as night in the desert. "The pharaoh gave it to her when she became a priestess." Mother was trying to hide something from me.

I still did not understand. "Grandfather give you new name?"

"No, but I am called Batya now."

I was confused. Batya was a Habiru name and meant "daughter of God."

"That is the name Yocheved gave me," Mother explained.

I was more confused. My sister, the Habiru, was a Khemetian priestess and had my mother's Khemetian name. My mother, the Khemetian, had a Habiru name given her by my and my sister's *ima*. And I, a Habiru, carried the name of an Egyptian god. I doubted I would ever understand.

Almah—for that is what I continued to call her—returned to the porch in answer to the chanting of her Khemetian name. Now, however, she wore a long white dress and looked like my sister. She turned and bowed to the pharaoh. In what even I knew was a remarkable gesture, he rose and bowed to her. The cheers and shouting of the crowd became so loud when he did that, I expected the pillars of the temple to crumble.

But Mother was not cheering, and when I happened to glance at Kakemour, there was a look of hatred and anger on his face that frightened me.

SOON AFTER I SAW Almah dance for the first time, Grandfather invited me and Mother to eat with him. This was not unusual, as we ate with him at least once a week, and sometimes more. Often it was just the three of us, but sometimes other children of his would be there. Some were adults, while others were my age or younger. I am not sure even Grandfather knows how many children he has. I asked Kakemour once and he said sixty, but that was five years ago. I wanted to ask him how many wives and concubines Grandfather had but was too shy. All the wives, concubines, and their children live in special palaces in various parts of Khemet and visit Grandfather when he asks them to, which is often. Grandfather likes women and children.

That afternoon when we went for dinner, we were surprised to see Almah sitting on the floor next to Grandfather as comfortably as a cat who knows she will not be punished regardless of what she does.

Mother looked somberly at Almah. If Ima was as silent as the river and Almah shone like polished sunlight, Mother was as serious as words on stone. Of my three mothers, she is the one who wants to understand everything. Ima and Almah have more in common than they will ever admit, because neither questions what she knows. Mother questions even when she knows. When Ima told stories about our ancestors, she told them the same way every time. Mother couldn't tell a story without wanting to know why Ya did such-and-such. Abba and Mother seemed like they didn't care if they found the answers as much as they were happy to look for them. Almah and Mother used to be like sisters. Now Mother was Ima's daughter, while Ima and her real daughter had not seen each other since before I learned to walk.

Something happened when Mother's mother, Queen Nefertari, died. I was still an infant then, but I remember Mother's grief felt like a calf being skinned while still alive. Even now, fifteen years later, when Mother talks about her mother, my stomach burns from cuts that have not healed.

I think Grandfather wanted Mother and Almah to be friends again, but they sat across from each other more wary than two strange cats being asked to drink milk from the same bowl. Silence at the dinner table was something no Khemetian could tolerate, and Grandfather broke it by asking me to recite a hymn to Osiris and to read to him from a papyrus of the Book of the Dead. I did, and he was delighted by how well I recited and read. It is odd that when I recite a poem or read from a scroll, my tongue feels as fluid as a fish moving through water. If only someone would always give me the right words to say.

After we finished eating, Grandfather said he wanted to show us something. "I apologize for not having shown it to you before," he said to Mother, "for having kept it a secret. I wanted to keep it to myself, and that was selfish."

Neither of us knew what he was talking about. As we left the dining room, Almah slipped her arm inside Grandfather's with no more thought than it took to blink one's eyes. I did not have to look up to know that Mother had noticed, too, and was wondering.

Mother and I followed them from the dining room, down a corridor, and into a small room I had never seen. One wall was covered with a painting of the goddess Maat kneeling, her feathered arms outstretched. Just as I wondered if this was what Grandfather had wanted us to see, Almah pushed against something on the back wall. A door opened. A secret room!

Mother and I looked at each other, then followed Almah and Grandfather through the door and into a room whose four white walls were covered with pictures of the most beautiful woman I had ever seen. Mother gasped loudly and I knew whom I was looking at. Or did I? I thought the paintings were of Queen Nefertari, but how amazing! They looked like Almah.

In one she was holding a baby, and I wondered if it was supposed to be Mother. In another she was sitting in the garden of the Women's Palace where Almah liked to sit, geese and ibises flying overhead. On another wall she walked in the garden of the palace at Opet with Ramesses. I had never known her, but looking at those paintings, oh, how I missed her!

I wished Ima could see this, because she says Khemetians are in love with death. But that is not true. It is just the opposite. They love life so much they cannot bear to believe it ends with death. Looking at the paintings of Nefertari, I agreed. It was not right or fair that someone so beautiful and gracious should be dead. And she wasn't. At least not in this secret room.

Grandfather stared for the longest at each painting, sometimes reaching out to touch her face lightly with his fingertips. Almah stood beside him, and I had the feeling they had come to the room many times. She seemed to know when Grandfather had stayed long enough because I was feeling grief like sand being blown against one's cheeks during a storm but could not tell if the grief belonged to Grandfather or Mother until Almah put her arm through his again and moved him gently away from the images of his beloved and toward the door. Mother was sobbing quietly, but I could not tell if it was from seeing the pictures of her mother, or that Almah had known about this room and she had not, or that it was Almah's hand her father was holding and not her own.

Almah stood at the threshold, looking at the walls covered with pictures of the woman she looked like. Suddenly music poured from her voice through barely parted lips, making me feel pain and joy as sharp-edged as the last sliver of color before night sits on the throne of heaven. There were no words, only soft notes of music searching for life and finding only shadows. Then she stopped and silence swallowed the last reverberation of melody, leaving each of us alone.

Chapter Two

ABBA'S HAIR AND BEARD are almost white now. His eyelids are puffy, and large folds of skin hang beneath his eyes, as if he has spent all his nights praying and his prayers have not been answered.

Abba sits on the couch next to me and takes a fig from the bowl offered him by a servant. Though I was not expecting him today, he has visited often in the three years since I've had my own suite. Sometimes he stays the night in Almah's suite down the hall because mine is small. Today, however, he has not come just to visit. Something is on his mind. I can't help wondering if he has come to ask me when I am going to acknowledge my true heritage and start working with him and Aharon. But that is probably just my guilt speaking. Ima might say that, but not Abba.

He chews noisily and I follow his eyes as he looks at the paintings on the walls. On the wall behind me is one of a crocodile with its mouth open, a reminder to me of the miracle of my life. To a Khemetian, however, it is a depiction of the god Sobek. Over Abba's shoulder is a scene of three women playing with a child, the only way I have devised of bringing my three mothers together. On the wall by the door leading to my bedroom a woman dances. It is not Almah, but that is who I think of when I look at it.

"So," Abba says in Habiru, his eyes finally coming to rest on my face, "why have you stopped coming to visit your mother?"

His words take me by surprise. I feel myself blushing. "Long time," I finally manage to say.

"Do you know how long?" Abba insists.

I do. I look down at the floor.

"How do you think your mother feels? It has been a year since her last-born child has been to see her. A year! Aharon and Miryam think you don't like them. Your mother is afraid you have become a traitor to your people. Like your sister."

My mouth moves as I search for an excuse, but not even the sound of anguish comes out. I have no excuse. How can I tell Abba that I do not like being around Ima, that I never have? Only Almah understands what it is like to be with your real mother and wish you were with almost anyone else in the world. I know I am not supposed to have these feelings and I wish I didn't. But I do.

Abba sighs and takes another fig from the bowl the servant left on the table. After more noisy chewing, he resumes talking. "I know you are not a traitor. Neither is your sister. But only you and I believe that. You remember the story of our forefather Yitzchak, his wife, Rivka, and their two sons, Yaakov and Esav?"

Of course. When Rivka was pregnant, Ya told her she was carrying twin boys and the one born first, Esav, would serve the younger twin, Yaakov. Years passed. Yitzchak was old and blind and thought he was going to die. He wanted to give Esav the inheritance, but Rivka found out. She disguised Yaakov to be like Esav, and Yitzchak gave Yaakov the inheritance by mistake.

"Sometimes one parent sees something in a child the other does not," Abba continues. "Parents have favorites. Avraham favored Yitzchak over Yishmael. Rivka favored Yaakov over Esav, and Yaakov favored Yosef over his other eleven sons. It is not right, but sometimes a parent sees himself in a child, or sees himself as he would like to be. Most of the time it is the child who looks at the parents and sees who he wants to be. But occasionally the parent lives through the child. Yitzchak was quiet; Esav was a hunter, a man of the outdoors, and that was the kind of man Yitzchak would have liked to have been. Because of that he could not see that Esav was not the one to whom he should pass responsibility for the knowledge of Ya, the one god, the god who cannot be seen because he is the creator of all the gods who can be seen. This was what the inheritance was. If Esav had received it, there would be no Habiru today. That is why Rivka tricked her husband. She knew a truth he did not."

Abba shakes his head. "The more white there is in my hair and beard, the less I understand. The more weariness in my eyes, the more I question whether I have made the right decisions."

He gets up and begins pacing slowly. "Yocheved blames me. She says if I had not taught Almah to speak Khemetian, things would be different. That is true. If I had not taught her Khemetian, she would not have been able to speak to the princess and you would not have been saved from the soldiers. However, if I had not taught her Khemetian, she would be living in Goshen, married, and teaching her children about Ya. But I saw something in your sister your mother did not."

"What?" I ask.

"The spark of holiness!"

I would not have thought of those words, but I think I understand.

"When I was a boy," he goes on, "my father would wake me to go to the roof with him and say the morning prayers as the sun rose. That is how his father taught him and how I thought I would teach my son. But my first child was a daughter. Maybe everything would be different if I had thought a woman could pray to Ya like a man. It never occurred to me.

"One morning as I came onto the roof, Almah was already there. She was only four or five. Her back was to me and she was facing east. I was about to say something, when she opened her arms as if commanding the sun to rise. And just then, it did, and its first rays flowed over her like a water of light. She stood perfectly still, her arms outstretched as if—as if she were a goddess. I could not believe I had such a thought, but she reminded me of paintings on the walls of the temples in Pi-Ramesses.

"When she lowered her arms I went to her and asked, 'What game were you playing?'

"She looked at me seriously and said, 'I wasn't playing.'

"I didn't ask her anything else. I didn't want to know. I never saw her do it again, and I came to the rooftop late for several mornings after that to watch her. But she was never there, though she wasn't asleep, either. I suspected she had found another place, a secret one, known only to her and the sun. That was when I began speaking to her in Khemetian. I don't know why I did. It seemed like the right thing, and the rapidity with which she learned made me wonder if Khemetian was really her first tongue."

I see a smile of pride on his lips as he relives the scene with his firstborn. Then he looks at me and his eyes shine with the avidity of conviction. "What I saw in Almah that morning was the courage to love holiness. Do you know how rare that is? It is one thing to follow all the rules that are supposed to make you holy. It is another to hug holiness to you. Yocheved *believes* in Ya and the special destiny he has promised our people. But she does not *love* the mystery of the sun rising. Your sister did. I had no idea what it meant. But I was convinced it was not wrong. As surely as Rivka knew that Yaakov was the true heir, I knew Almah understood holiness in a way I could not begin to imagine."

I nodded and glanced at the painting of the woman dancing.

"Don't ever let your sister know, but I come to almost every festival to watch her dance. I am still uncomfortable seeing her without clothing, but after a while I forget she is my daughter. All I see is a goddess." He chuckles. "And I don't believe in goddesses. Or maybe I do and am afraid to say so. You see, I do not have Almah's courage to love. Maybe that is why she is my favorite. Please don't be hurt by that."

I shake my head. "Mine, too."

He smiles. "So, perhaps both of us seek to live courage through her."

I return his smile, though weakly because I am wondering if I will ever have my own courage.

Abba hesitates, as if there is something more he wants me to know but is not sure if I am ready to hear it or if he is ready to say it. "Could I have a cup of wine?" he asks.

I ring the bell that is on the floor beside the couch, and when the servant comes in, I ask for a jug of wine and a cup. Abba is silent until after the servant returns, pours the wine, and leaves. He takes a long sip, swallows, and sighs with satisfaction.

"One time in my life I had courage. I think. It was fifteen years ago, a few months after you, Almah, and your *ima* came to live here. One afternoon as Aharon and I were going back to Goshen after working in Pi-Ramesses, Yocheved was waiting on the road, looking for me. I had never seen her so upset. I sent your brother on and came with your mother and sat under a tree on the grass outside the palace walls.

"'You must do something about Almah,' she said. 'She has become the pharaoh's concubine.'

"I was shocked! My Almah? Yocheved swore it was true because the pharaoh had just that very morning given her baskets filled with golden bracelets, fine clothes, and a golden mirror that had belonged to his wife. And, if that were not bad enough, he had given her a suite of rooms of her own. 'No man gives a woman all that without expecting something in return.' She went on to say it was my fault that Almah refused to obey her any longer, so I had to make her go back to Goshen before it was too late.

"I refused to do anything until I talked to Almah. That made Yocheved even more angry. 'Don't you believe me?' she wanted to know. 'Don't you trust what I say?' I hate to say it, but the truth was I didn't trust Yocheved where Almah was concerned. I told her to get Almah.

"When Yocheved returned, a woman in a wig of long tight braids walked a few steps behind her. Her eyes, lips, and cheeks were painted, and golden bracelets were on her arms. She was wearing a dress of the finest linen, beneath which I could see the faintest outlines of her naked body. It was Almah! I couldn't believe my eyes, didn't want to believe them. Who knows what I would have done or said if Yocheved had not pointed at Almah and spat out, 'Here is the Pharaoh's whore!'

"Whatever shock and revulsion I may have felt looking at Almah, I knew as surely as I knew anything in my life that whatever Almah was doing or thought she was doing, she was not that. I looked at Almah. Her eyes were brimming with tears. I opened my arms and she rushed into them, and I held her to me as tightly as I could."

He stops and sips more wine. When he resumes, his voice cracks with pain suppressed. "Yocheved has never forgotten and never forgiven me. Fifteen years and she still looks at me as if I betrayed her. Perhaps I should not be telling you all this, but there is too much talk of Ya in our family and not enough about each other.

"I suppose I did betray her, but I *had* to protect Almah. Yocheved understands what it means to be obedient. She does not understand what it is to be a vessel for the holy. She pushed Almah out of my arms and shouted at her, 'If you do not go back to Goshen now, you will be dead to me. Your name will never pass my lips again, and I will not allow your name to be said in my presence. Choose. Ya or Pharaoh!'

"Though there were tears in Almah's eyes, there was also a calmness, the serenity of holiness. She looked at me. 'Which is it?' I asked her. Without thinking, I spoke to her in Khemetian. She answered, 'Look at me, Abba. Do you have to ask?'

"What was I supposed to have done? Was there something I could have done that would not have meant choosing my wife over my daughter, or my daughter over my wife? Fifteen years I have thought about that afternoon and have not found another answer. I looked at Yocheved and said, 'She chooses Pharaoh.' Yocheved's face muscles twitched as if I had slapped her.

"She didn't say a word but walked away from the palace and back to Goshen. She said the princess could get a wet nurse for you because that was all you needed her for. She and Almah have not seen each other since that day. Yocheved and I have never spoken of that afternoon, either. Nor have we spoken of much else. Fifteen years."

He is quiet for a long time. The light on the walls fades and a servant comes in to light the lamps.

Finally Abba continues. "To this day I do not know if I did the right thing. I have a daughter whose name is never mentioned. When the Teller recites the roll of the families and comes to the names of Amram and Yocheved and their children, Almah's name is not mentioned."

"Almah is good," I put in.

"But she is also a priestess of Hathor and Eset. We are Habiru and worship only Ya." Then he looks at me, his eyes as hard as hammered light. "And whom do you worship, Mosis?"

I shake my head and say nothing.

Chapter Three

ALMAH AND I HAVE DINNER together almost every night. Often she has to dance at a festival, attend a banquet with the pharaoh, or talk with a younger priestess who may be having a problem, so it will be late before she returns. But I am always here waiting for her. When I awake each morning, I like knowing that my day will end with Almah.

I am most myself when we are together because then I come closest to saying what I feel. Even if she does not always understand, she takes my words into her heart as if they were the notes of a bird's song at dawn. I do not have trouble talking when Almah is listening. I tell her about Abba's visit but leave out that he has seen her dance.

"How do you feel about going back to see Ima? Do you want to?" she wants to know, biting into a date.

"I never want to see Goshen again as long as I live. I hated it all those years Mother took me there once a week or so to visit. I hate to say it, but I don't have pleasant memories of Ima. She seems to enjoy seeing me forced to eat from straw bowls and dishes and speak Habiru. Both she and Mother were always telling me how important it was to get to know 'my people.' I don't have any 'people.' I feel closer to the servants and court officials and scribes. Aharon is less of an older brother to me than Kakemour, who taught me to use a bow and arrow, swords, a spear, and how to drive a horse and chariot."

Almah smiles sadly. "I am sorry it is so hard for you."

"You don't know how much I envy you," I say with anguish. "You haven't had to go to Goshen in fifteen years nor listen to Ima go on and on about Ya."

She nods. "That's true, but sometimes I miss her. She is my mother. Sometimes I wish she could see me dance even though she would hate it and me for doing it. Still, I think someplace deep down inside she would be proud of me, too." Almah laughs sadly. "No. I am wishing for something that will never be. That is not Ima. That is the *ima* I wish she were."

"Odd family," I say, and we laugh. "Think about it," I continue. "You were born Habiru but are so accepted by the Khemetians that people refer to me as often by the title Brother of the Priestess as they do Grandson of the Pharaoh. Mother, born Khemetian, is more accepted in Goshen than either you or I. She speaks fluent Habiru now and almost looks like one since she stopped wearing jewelry and makeup."

"But she won't let her hair grow out," Almah puts in, chuckling.

"No. Said she couldn't—yet. But she speaks of Ya as if he is her god."

"And who is your god, Mosis?" Almah asks quietly.

We are lying at opposite ends of a couch, our legs touching lightly, each of us cupping a bowl of sweet wine as the servants take away the dishes.

I shake my head. "Don't want to talk about it."

"I know. But perhaps you will know who you are once you know which god you serve."

I want to ask her something, but I am afraid of how I will feel if she does not say what I want to hear. But I have to know. I wonder if I will be able to serve any god until I do know.

"What's the matter?" she asks after the silence has gone on too long.

I look at her and then look away.

"Talk to me, Mosis."

"I'm afraid of what you might say."

"Might say about what?"

"Might say if I decide to serve Ya." My voice sounds so small in my ears I am not certain I have said anything aloud.

But I know I have when I hear Almah say, "Mosis, we don't have to agree for me to love you. I want you to be as happy serving the god you want to as I am serving the ones I do."

"Thank you. Thank you so much."

"Is that what you want to do? Serve Ya?"

I shake my head. "Don't know. That's the problem! Look at me. My eyelids are painted. My body is oiled. Gold bracelets on my wrists. It's ridiculous, but I feel naked if I don't have on jewelry. I like living here in the palace and going to banquets with Kakemour and meeting beautiful women. I enjoy that more than visiting Ima and hearing boring stories. And yet, you belong here. I don't. But I don't belong there, either."

She nods eagerly. "I do know what you mean. It is only because I belong to the goddess that I feel at home here. But otherwise, I feel somewhat like a stranger, too."

"But what about the pharaoh? You seem to be the one he wants closest to him. Almah?" I stop. There is something else I have been wanting to ask her for almost as long as I can remember. "Almah?"

"What is it, Mosis?"

"Do you— Have you—?"

She smiles. "No, I do not sleep with Ramesses. I never have. He wanted to make me his wife once."

"Are you serious?" I exclaim. "You might have been Great Royal Wife? Why didn't you?"

"I don't know if he would have made me Great Royal Wife. But Ramesses did not need to make me his wife to help him assuage his grief for Nefertari. He loves me, yes. But what he loves more is looking at me and seeing her. What woman wants to live as a substitute for one who is dead? No, I belong to the goddess, and that is why the people love me so. Because no man can have me, then I belong to everyone—men and women. But sometimes I wish you and I were truly Khemetian and had been born into the royal family. Then we could marry each other."

I blush.

"I'm sorry. Maybe I shouldn't have said that."

"No. No. I'm glad you did. I've thought it enough

times." Still, I am not comfortable talking about it anymore and look for a way to change the subject. "But all we've done is talk about me. What about you? How're things with you?"

"Well, I'm not sure. I mean, I'm fine, but maybe I should tell you and see what you think."

"About what?"

"For the past week or so I have been feeling that Intef, Kakemour, and Ramesses are planning something, and they want to keep it a secret from me. Whenever I enter the throne room, they stop talking. That has never happened. Maybe it's nothing. But I don't like it, Mosis. I thought they trusted me. Now I am not sure, and it hurts."

"You are worried."

"Yes, I am. I have to find out what they're planning. Maybe you can help."

"How?" I ask, unable to think of what I could do.

"I know I'm probably being silly, but would you talk to Batya? She might know something. Would you talk to her?"

"Of course, but what could she know?"

"Probably nothing, but I don't know what else to do."

THE NEXT MORNING Mother appears just as I am finishing breakfast. We embrace. She looks at me and I at her because we have not seen each other in a long time. I had almost forgotten how much I love this face from which goodness shines like fire.

"It has been too long," she says hesitantly, sitting on a couch.

"Yes."

"How have you been?"

She is the only person I know who asks that question in such a way that you know she is not inquiring about your physical well-being.

I shake my head. "I am not sure."

"What's the matter?"

"I'm fifteen. No wife. No children. I don't do anything. I don't fit anywhere. If Grandfather died, I would be thrown into the street. Look at me! I walk and talk and dress like a Khemetian, but I am not. You are more Habiru than I am!"

"Mosis." Her voice is quiet, but there is so much strength in it. When I was little I believed that if she spoke to a crocodile, it would close its jaws and ask her to forgive it for being a crocodile. "Yocheved and I have wondered, too, wondered why Ya would want a Habiru boy brought up in the palace of the pharaoh."

"Do you know?"

"I may. I just may."

"Tell me, please."

"Do you ever think about your ancestor Yosef?"

"No. Not really."

"Perhaps you should. He was even more lonely than you. You have always known your family. He was taken from his when he was seventeen and sold into Khemet as a slave. He rose to become the second most powerful man in all the land. And yet he never forgot Ya. He never forgot he was Habiru. There was no one to remind him of this. Yet he remembered."

She does not have to say the rest: I have forgotten. I drop my head to my chest.

"I am glad your *ka* is troubled," she continues. "I was afraid I would come to you and you would not want to listen. But a troubled *ka* wants peace and will listen to anything that may bring that peace."

I look up at her. "What do you mean?"

"Perhaps the time has come for us to find out why Ya wanted you raised as the grandson of Ramesses. But I am not comfortable talking to you where Kakemour or someone else might come in. Come to my apartment in the Women's Palace this afternoon during the time when Ramesses, Kakemour, and Intef always listen to petitions."

Almah was right. Something is going on. Mother knows what it is and thinks I can do something. I am excited but also frightened. What if I cannot live up to her expectations? What if she thinks I am capable of more than I am? What if Ya expects too much of me?

As I go down the broad staircase to make my usual morning appearance in the throne room, I am nervous. However, no one is whispering conspiratorially and neither does anyone pay attention to me. The scribes and priests greet me without a second glance. Grandfather, Intef, and Kakemour are going over the list of those who want audiences with the pharaoh this afternoon.

I used to sit next to Grandfather and listen to the

problems people brought for him to solve. Sometimes he would lean toward me, instead of Intef on his right, and ask what I thought he should do. I would tell him and, to my surprise, sometimes he agreed and would do the opposite of what he had planned.

Once a woman, the wife of a priest, had a child that was not the priest's. The woman claimed the child was a gift of the gods. The priest said the child belonged to another man. Grandfather believed the priest. Then, more out of fun than any sense that I might have something to say, he asked me what I thought. I said, "To believe the priest might undermine belief in the powers of the gods. If belief in the gods' powers is weakened, might that not affect yours?"

He looked at me sharply with those small piercing eyes of his. Then he turned to Kakemour. "And what does the next *tjat* think?"

"I would ask Mosis what would happen if many women suddenly had children by the gods? Would that not undermine *maat*?"

"Excellent question," Ramesses affirmed. "Mosis?"

"If it does, maybe the gods are not happy with the men."

Ramesses laughed loudly. "With a mind that subtle, you could be a dangerous man to have for an enemy, Mosis."

I noticed that neither Kakemour nor Intef laughed.

During the past year I have become uncomfortable watching people's happiness being decided by one man—sometimes me. Grandfather says, "It is *maat* we serve,

Mosis. Divine order. Every decision must increase *maat* and decrease *isfet*, 'chaos and injustice.'"

How does he know what is *maat* and what is *isfet*? I asked him once to give me a list so I would know which is which.

"It is not always that clear," he said.

"So how do you know?"

"I just do."

I don't know if that was the real answer or he couldn't tell me. Maybe the knowledge is imparted to him each morning when the priests bathe him in water mixed with saltwort and shave his entire body with a golden razor, plucking any remaining hairs with golden tweezers. Maybe the knowledge is in the oil they rub over his body or in the sacrifice he offers to the gods while the priests sing prayers and read to him from the sacred literature. Or perhaps not.

I used to enjoy looking down at the people as they kiss the ground at our feet. Now I am uneasy. Perhaps it is because Grandfather seems to have stopped listening to the people when they come with their problems. Even I am beginning to feel that they all sound alike, and I have to remind myself that the *people* with the problems are not alike. But Grandfather interrupts people now and gives decisions though he has not heard everything they came to say. He didn't used to be that way.

Just as I gradually stopped going to Goshen, I gradually stayed away from hearing cases. Even though I still appear each morning to pay my respects to Grandfather, I am sorry now that I have not been around as much. If I had been, I might know what they are planning, if anything. All I can do is wait impatiently for the afternoon.

IT HAS BEEN THREE YEARS since I moved from the Women's Palace, and I have had no reason to return until now, since Mother is seldom here anymore. Whichever concubines Ramesses wants near him live in the palace with their children. All of them want to be named Great Royal Wife, but no one has borne that title since Nefertari. I would be surprised if anyone ever did again.

More than any other place, however, this is home. It is where I lived for the first twelve years of my life, minus the three months or so when I was silent in Goshen. As I walk in I gaze at the paintings on both sides of the hallway and am pleased that the ibises and hawks are still on their eternal flight, that the catfish has not yet been killed by the spear aimed at its side, that the arrow in Ramesses's bow has not yet been launched at the lion to the right of his chariot. I can see myself running through the hallways chasing or being chased by whatever children of Ramesses were around at the time. It is good to be here, to remember that there was a time when I was happy, when I was who I appeared to be.

As I go up the staircase to the second floor and Mother's apartment, some of the servants recognize me and bow. I smile and greet them by name, pleased that I remember them, too. They still think that I am who I appear to be. Why isn't that enough for me?

Mother is seated on a couch as I come in, and she watches me as I look around and remember.

"What are you thinking?" she wants to know.

"Kittens should not become cats. I was happier when I was a kitten here."

Mother smiles wistfully. "Come. Sit. Perhaps the time has come when you can find happiness in being a cat."

I sit down, wishing she would tell me stories about when I was a child here. But she is even more serious than normal and begins talking immediately.

"As you know, next year will be Ramesses's thirtieth year as Pharaoh. Naturally, he wants to make it a year people will remember for a long time. But all is not going well. The Temple to Amon-Re being built in Pi-Ramesses was supposed to have been finished before the harvest. It will not be finished by this time next year unless something is done. Now that the harvest is almost over, Ramesses has decided to send soldiers into Goshen and force every Habiru—women, children, and old people—to work on the temple. That is the only way it can be finished in time."

"What?" I exclaim in disbelief. "That is not like Grandfather. He has always treated the Habiru like any other workers—Khemetian, Nubian, Midianite, or whomever. Is he also going to force their women, children, and old people to work on the temple?"

"No. Just the Habiru."

"This is a kind of slavery!" I exclaim.

"Yocheved says they have always been slaves. Only now it seems Ramesses is going to make them feel it. But I am not sure this was his idea. Asetnefret is eager to have the new temple finished because she wants to be married in it. Ramesses is going to make her Great Royal Wife."

"Asetnefret?" The name is familiar, but I can't place it.

"She was Second Royal Wife. After Mother died, Asetnefret disappeared. Quite frankly, I hoped Ramesses had had her killed. Unfortunately, that is not the case. She has been living at the Harem Palace in the Land of the Lakes, where he sent her after Mother died. She blames Almah because if Almah had not looked so much like Nefertari, Father would have made Asetnefret Great Royal Wife many years ago. He saw her on one of his visits a few years ago and, over time, she has managed to win his favor again. Even though Ramesses has more than thirty concubines and eighty children, he is lonely."

I remember now. Asetnefret hates Habiru. "How do you know all this, Mother?"

"I was sitting in the garden yesterday and Kakemour saw me. In the course of talking, he told me."

"How . . . how did he seem? I mean, was he pleased about Ramesses's decision?"

"He wasn't displeased," she responds after thinking about it. "But that's not important. The reason I have told you all this is because I think this is why Ya wanted you raised as the pharaoh's grandson."

"What do you mean?" I am hoping she doesn't think I can stop what is going to happen. "What . . . what can I do?" I ask her, my voice shaking.

"I don't know, but you must do something. How could you live with yourself if you didn't?"

I look at this woman I have always called Mother, though I have always known I did not enter this world through her body. For the first time, I see her as a woman apart—Meryetamun, daughter of Pharaoh, who has become Batya, daughter of God. She changed my life by bringing me to grow up in this palace, but I understand, also for the first time, that her life has been changed even more profoundly. If she had known what was going to happen, would she have picked that baby up out of the basket? I think she would have. The question is, if I had known what was going to happen, would I have let her?

I don't think so. What is she asking of me? Does she want me to tell Grandfather not to do what he is about to do? I may be his grandson, so to speak, but he is a god. Whether I believe that is not important. He believes it, and so does everyone else. There is nothing I can do, and I wish Mother would not act as if there were.

"Mother?"

"Yes."

"What are you going to do?"

"I think I will let my hair grow," she says simply. "I have tried to live in two worlds, but if Ramesses does this, then I choose to be Habiru. I would rather be with those who suffer than with those who cause suffering."

I am shocked and do not know what to say except no, Mother. Don't. If she chooses, it means I, too, will have to choose and I don't want to.

Mother looks around the room. "I have no place here anymore. I have not had a place here for three years now, since you moved to the main palace. Now that you are grown, I have nothing to do. I have no reason to remain here. In Goshen it is different."

"What's different?"

"I am the daughter Yocheved wanted Almah to be and the big sister Miryam wanted. And I no longer believe Taweret gave you to me. I am ashamed that I could ever have believed in a goddess with the body of a hippo and the head of a lion."

"And Almah thinks it is ridiculous to believe in a god you cannot touch or see."

"What do you believe, Mosis?"

I shake my head. "That is what Almah asked me. Abba, too."

"And what did you say?"

"I asked Almah a question. And perhaps I will ask it of you."

"What is it?"

"Will you love me if I want to serve Taweret, Hathor, Amon-Re, and all the others?"

She pauses for a long time, almost too long, I think, but then she says, finally, "It would not be easy, but yes— yes, I would. Mosis? Is that what you want to do, serve the gods of Egypt?"

I shake my head. "I don't know, Mother."

She smiles weakly. "I'm glad."

Chapter Four

DAYS PASS. Nothing happens. Then, one morning as I walk into the throne room, all heads turn toward the door and everyone is suddenly silent and still. There are no smiles and nods of recognition. No one even bothers to greet me. Though I have often felt like a stranger here among these men, this is the first time I feel unwelcome and unwanted.

Normally I would walk across this huge room to where Grandfather sits in his throne chair, but he is not there this morning. Only Intef, who comes rapidly toward me and puts his arm around my shoulders. My body stiffens. He has never touched me and I do not think I want the feel of his touch now, but I do nothing to dislodge his arm.

"The pharaoh thinks it would be better if you did not come to the throne room for a while, or be seen about too much," he says quietly, turning me away from the room and starting to walk me back toward the door. "It has been necessary to force the Habiru to work on the new temple so it will be ready in time for the pharaoh's marriage to Asetnefret. Although the pharaoh has no doubts about your loyalty, there may be others here at court who wonder if you would be able to give your full support. Rather than risk any confrontations, the pharaoh thinks it wiser if you are not seen about for a while."

Intef has walked me rapidly into the hallway, and before I can say anything, he has turned and gone back inside. My face is burning with the heat of shame. Why didn't Grandfather tell me himself? Why did he wait until I came to see him? Why didn't he send someone to my suite this morning—or come himself? And where is Kakemour? He could have come and told me. But no! I am left to stand here while people hurry in and out of the throne room. Yesterday they greeted me: "In peace! In peace, Mosis, grandson of the pharaoh!" Today they walk past me as if I do not exist. Today I feel as if the very walls and floors were thinking *Mosis the Habiru!*

Tears are running down my face, but I do not care who sees. They may look like tears of hurt and sorrow—and I suppose several of them are—but most are tears of rage! But I do not know if I am angry at all those who knew me yesterday and will not speak with me today, angry at Grandfather for being afraid to tell me himself, or angry at myself for having played the game of Pharaoh's grandson. I am such a fool! Such a fool in my gold bracelets and perfumed wig and oiled body!

I run down the hall to the stairway leading up to the living quarters on the third floor, where I burst into

Almah's suite without knocking. The main room is empty and I am about to hurry out, when I see her standing on the balcony.

"Almah!"

She does not turn around. I go and stand beside her as my gaze follows hers. We are high enough here to see to the river, and there, on the Avenue of the Pharaoh, I see them, thousands of them—Habiru men, women, children, old people—walking toward Pi-Ramesses, soldiers standing almost shoulder to shoulder on each side.

I look at her and am surprised to see tears flowing down her face. Without a word we fall into each other's arms and hold each other tightly. Eventually we separate and go inside and sit in our usual positions on the couch. When we finally speak, it is in Habiru.

"I suppose, deep down, I was hoping Ramesses would change his mind," she says sadly. "I honestly didn't believe he would do this, not even after you told me what Batya said."

"Neither did I."

"Even so, as close as we are—or as close as I assumed we were—I would have thought he would have told me."

"He didn't say anything to you?" I exclaim incredulously.

"No. He didn't say anything to you?"

"When I went to the throne room a while ago, I was met with the silence of the dead. Intef told me not to come there anymore, or be seen around the palace, because they don't think I fully support what the pharaoh is doing."

"In other words, you are suspected of being disloyal, a traitor."

I nod, angry tears pooling in my eyes again.

"No one has told me anything. I didn't know a thing until I stepped out on the balcony this morning and saw the soldiers and the people. I couldn't believe my eyes. I almost didn't do the morning ritual today, but I knew that would make me look suspicious. And the goddess might not like it. When I got to the temple, I noticed the other priests and priestesses looking at me, trying to see if I knew, but I acted as if everything were normal. And when I went to see Ramesses, he was nowhere to be found."

"I think he is so ashamed that he doesn't know what to say to either of us."

"That is probably true," she agrees. "All of this was Asetnefret's idea. I know it!"

"How can you be sure?"

She sighs. "I probably shouldn't tell you this, but I think you need to know. When I was on my way from the temple to the palace this morning, I saw Kakemour. I was surprised because he is not usually out so early. But there he was, wearing his soldier's kilt and carrying a sword. 'Off to kill more Habiru babies?' I asked."

"You didn't?" I put in, incredulous and proud of my sister.

"I did."

"What did he say?"

"He turned red but more from anger than embarrassment, I think. But when he spoke . . . Well, for the first time in my life, I was afraid. He said, 'A piece of advice,

Priestess. I would be careful not to repeat such a comment. Habiru sympathizers will be thrown into prison. Even those who speak Khemetian as if they really are.' He was not hostile. Just matter-of-fact. That is what made it so frightening. Then he went on to tell me that at the same time the pharaoh marries Asetnefret, he, Kakemour, will be married to the youngest daughter of the pharaoh and Asetnefret. 'My interest in seeing the temple completed on time is a personal one, which is why I have been put in charge of seeing that it happens.'"

I don't understand. How could Kakemour, who is like a brother to me, marry the daughter of a woman who he knows hates Habiru? How could he do that? I loved him more than the brother of my blood.

"I don't understand," I say. "I don't understand how Grandfather and Kakemour could love us and yet do this. Did they love us in spite of our being born Habiru? Or were they able to love us only by pretending that we were not born Habiru?"

She shakes her head. "I don't think it's either. I think they always saw us as Meryetamun and Mosis. Two individuals. When they started plotting to put the Habiru into slavery, then they remembered that we are not only Meryetamun and Mosis, and suddenly their love for us is very confusing."

"I don't want to live like this anymore, Almah. I'm tired of thinking about who I am and what my place is. I keep thinking about going to Goshen. You know, it doesn't matter how they look at me or what they think about me there. They have to take me in because I, too, am a descendant of Avraham and Sarah, Yitzchak and Rivka, Yaakov, Rachel, and Leah. And I am the son of Amram and Yocheved."

I stop my pacing and look at her, but she is staring into her lap. The shadows of loneliness are deep in her face. I go to her and put my arms around her. "Almah? Come with me? Go back to Goshen with me? It might be hard at first, but we could make it work. We could! I know we could!" I would leave all this right now if Almah would come with me!

She disengages herself gently from my arms, and takes my face in the palms of her hands and looks at me. "The thought of losing you fills me with more fear than I know how to contain, Mosis. If marriage is two feelings becoming one feeling, then I am more married to you than I could be to any man. A woman is never truly married until her husband takes her away emotionally from her father and her brothers. It is easy to move her into another house, but feelings weigh more than a chair and no man could ever take you away from me."

Her hands drop from my face and I break into a smile. "Then it's settled!" I exclaim, getting up from the couch. "We will return to Goshen."

"No," she says immediately. "It is only because I love you so much that I can let you go. For you there is no other choice. You have no life here. I would have no life there."

"There would be something you could do," I plead.

"I belong to the goddess, Mosis. If I am going to pray to a god, and I must pray, then I'd rather it be a woman. Ya does not know how to receive my nakedness."

"Have you ever danced naked before Ya? How do you know? Maybe he's just waiting for a woman to dance naked for him." I know I am being ridiculous, but I will say anything, anything I can think of to convince her to come with me.

"Even when I was little, I had trouble with Ya. Who was he? Where was he? I remember the very first time I came to Pi-Ramesses. I couldn't have been more than two or three, but I remember the statues of all the gods and goddesses, and I knew then that being born something doesn't mean that's what you are. I didn't know that in words, but when Abba started teaching me Khemetian, it was the first time I felt like words belonged to me. These were words my mouth liked the feel of. And every little thing he told me about Khemet made sense. Why would a woman worship a male god like Ya when she can worship females like Eset and Hathor? Women need to see things and touch them. Ima has only one god. Maybe that's how men see things—men and the women who agree with them—but to me, as a woman, the world is too big and too complex. How can one god take care of everything for everybody? Having many gods and goddesses makes more sense.

"I'm sorry, Mosis, but I can't go back to Goshen. I know who I am here, even though I hate what Ramesses and Kakemour are doing—even though my own life may be in danger now that Asetnefret has returned to power. But this is the life I chose. This is the life I want. What I chose for me is not what you should choose for you."

She stands up and hugs me tightly. "I have to go to the temple for my midmorning ritual bath."

"I don't want to go without you," I say, and start to cry.

"Shhhh," she says softly, putting a finger to my lips.

And she hurries from the room, but not before I see the tears brimming in her eyes as I break into loud sobbing.

Chapter Five

I DO NOT KNOW HOW LONG I stay in Almah's suite. I am afraid to leave because, if I do, I may never see it or her again. But I am also afraid to be here when she comes back. Finally, when my eyes dry, I hurry down the hallway, hoping not to see anyone. Yet the hallway is empty, as if no one wants to see me, either.

I don't know what to do. Grandfather wants me to stay in here, see no one, and be seen by no one until the temple is completed; but that will be months. And how do I know life will return to normal after that? What if he decides he wants the Habiru to build him *another* temple?

I told Almah that I wanted to live in Goshen, but I would not make a good slave. I have never worked a day in my life, or had someone order me around, telling me what to do and when to do it. I wouldn't know how to take orders, and I don't want to learn. I am fooling myself if I think I could live in Goshen.

So what am I supposed to do? I will not be a slave, and if I stay here I will be a prisoner, or worse—a person whose life has no meaning in anyone's eyes, not even my own.

I go over it again and again in my mind. There has to be another choice. But if there is, I can't find it. Finally I am tired of thinking and tired of being confused. I need to get out of here, get some air, feel the sun on my body. But where can I go? I can't sit in Grandfather's garden, something I would do normally. I could go into Pi-Ramesses, but I'm not sure that's a good idea. I didn't go out during harvesttime because I was afraid of what I would see. Things are no better now.

But maybe that is what I should do. Go and see for myself. Maybe I'll find out that being a slave isn't as bad as I think it is. Or maybe it'll be worse. Either way, I will know where I want to be. And if I know that, then I'll know *who* I want to be.

SOLDIERS LINE THE Avenue of the Pharaoh on both sides, hands gripping their upraised spears as their eyes search the crowd for any untoward movement. The threat of death mingles with the smell of the lambs and cows being herded to the market. At the riverside I see Habiru men, women, and children unloading blocks of stone from barges, to load them on carts, which others pull toward the temple site in town.

The soldiers are outnumbered by the Habiru, who could attack the soldiers and take their spears and swords. But the Habiru do not seem to notice. They don't even look angry or resentful about what is happening to them.

I allow myself to be taken along with the crowds—Nubians, Lybians, Midianites, Syrians, Khemetians, and Habiru—toward where the new temple is being built. I do not like being jostled and bumped with almost every step I take, but I act as if I do not notice.

Finally I arrive at the temple building site. There is no doubt Ramesses will be remembered as the greatest builder in history. When I was small I remember being impressed by the temples—the scenes carved into the walls, the height of the columns. Today it does not make sense, especially when I think that I am supposed to be one of those men pulling that huge block of stone up the ramp. What would my life mean if this is all it was? Ramesses will be remembered throughout time, but his muscles will not ache from having moved even one stone. While all these whose muscles cry out for rest will be as nameless as grains of sand.

"Well, what a surprise!"

I recognize the voice and turn to see Kakemour, a big smile on his face, walking toward me down the broad temple steps. "So, what brings you into Pi-Ramesses?"

Despite myself I am glad to see him. His and Almah's faces have been more constant in my life than any others. It was easier to believe bad things about him when I couldn't see his smile. Seeing him now I am ashamed that I could have had a negative thought about him. I shrug. "Get away. Get outside."

He nods sympathetically. "Yes. I know. I am sorry it has to be that way for a while." He is holding a whip idly by his side.

"Why?" I want to know. "What is going on? One day everything normal. The next, I am not trusted."

Kakemour's face turns red. "We can't be too careful. Believe me. I argued with the queen—well, the soon-to-be queen. I told her you had lived in the palace every day of your life, practically. She said it would be safer if you kept a low profile until the temple is finished. She said it would be understandable if you had feelings about the necessity of forcing the Habiru to work. She wanted to spare you both the sight of it as well as minimize any risk that you might do something foolish."

"Such as?"

"Well, it would be understandable if you wanted to do something to help your parents and siblings. *I* know you wouldn't incite the Habiru against the pharaoh, but Asetnefret doesn't like to take chances."

Me? Incite someone? So, that's what this is about. Even though I grew up in the palace and Khemetian is my first tongue and I look Khemetian, they think of me as Habiru. Mother was right! This is all the doing of Asetnefret. "Grandfather?" I ask hesitantly, wanting to know what he said.

Kakemour looks away, as if something a worker is doing has caught his eye, but he doesn't want to look at me, doesn't want to see me looking at him.

"He thought it was a good idea. It's not that he doesn't trust you. No, no. Nothing like that. But you know the inner workings of the palace, where the horses and chariots are kept, the routines of the guards, all of which is valuable information. What if some Habiru hotheads decide to organize a rebellion? They could kidnap you, torture you, and you would have no choice but to tell them everything you know about palace life. I'm sure that no one will mind your being here today, but if you come into the city on too many more days, that might arouse suspicion."

Anger rises in me slowly like the river when the floods are beginning. They do not trust either of us. They have never accepted me as one of them. I am tolerated but I do not belong.

Kakemour tries to smile. "What are you worrying about these things for? It is not for the likes of men like you and me to get too involved in such heavy matters."

He is trying to appease me, but he insults my intelligence. He is the future *tjat* and son-in-law to the pharaoh. This is precisely the kind of thing he must be involved in. When Kakemour goes to put his arm around me as if we are going for a chariot ride or to take a boat onto the river and hunt ducks, I know he is not taking me seriously and I brush his arm off. "I'm not a child! Talk to me like an adult!"

The smile leaves his face so suddenly I wonder if it was really there. "Very well. You want to know the truth. No one wants to hurt your feelings. I don't, either, but you're right. You're not a child any longer. You deserve the truth."

There is a hardness in the center of his eyes that I have never seen. Or maybe I simply never noticed.

"I have always wondered whose side you would be on," he says calmly. "When you and your sister first came to live here, I tried to explain to her, once, why Kheme-tians do not trust Habiru, can never trust Habiru. Nothing has changed. Queen Asetnefret is right. She was right fifteen years ago when Meryetamun took leave of her senses and brought you here. And if Queen Nefertari had not died when she did, Queen Asetnefret would have had her way."

I look at him sharply and he stops. I have to ask him. I have to know. "That night. Fifteen years ago. Would you have killed me?" I stop, but my eyes bore into his until he explodes in anger.

"How dare you ask me that! Do you not understand that nothing is more important than *maat*? But that is a concept no Habiru can grasp, not even you, who grew up with it. How can you trust a people who speak another language and worship another god? In an emergency—and this is an emergency—where does their loyalty lie? You grew up in the pharaoh's palace as his grandson, but your *ka* is still Habiru."

"No!" I shout back. "I am loyal to Ramesses. But this"—and my arms fling out to embrace the Habiru working—"no!"

Kakemour shakes his head "No, Mosis! No! There is only one issue. Building this temple to the glory of Amon-Re and Pharaoh. Nothing else matters. But perhaps you do not believe that the sun rises each day only because of the pharaoh's rituals and prayers. Perhaps you do not really believe the pharaoh is a god who has taken on human form and there is nothing greater than his presence in our midst. Look around you, Mosis! Look at these people working here, people from all over the world. All of them pay homage to Pharaoh. Look, Mosis! Many of those working here are Khemetians! We did not have to send soldiers to get them to come work. Old and young! When they heard that more workers were needed to complete the temple on time, they volunteered—women, children, old people. For them it is an honor to work here. 'Tell me what I can do!' they wanted to know. Only the Habiru had to be forced. Yet the pharaoh permits the Habiru to live on the richest land in all Khemet. But when the pharaoh needs them for something, not only do they not come voluntarily, when they are forced to come, they act like they are being marched to their deaths. You think I am cruel. I think the Habiru are ungrateful. I would not want to have the same opinion of you."

I have never seen him so angry. The short whip is trembling in his hand as if his emotions are more than his body can contain. With a shock I realize that he wants to hit me and would do so if he were sure Grandfather would not be angry.

But why? Why is he so angry that he would whip me if he could? Because he thinks I am ungrateful? But ungrateful for what? I did not ask to be raised in the pharaoh's palace. Yes, I am glad that Ya or Taweret decided that I would, but has Kakemour been merely doing me a favor all these years? Maybe that is it. Maybe I was never his little brother as much as I was a duty he had to carry out as future *tjat*. Maybe Grandfather told him to be like a brother to me. Otherwise he would not have done it.

"So, you don't have anything to say, Mosis?"

The thing that would satisfy me now would be to snatch the whip from his hand and slash him across the face. And that would not be good, so I shake my head and back away, stumbling against someone who pushes me off him and into the crowd.

All day I let the throngs of people push me in this direction and that, as if I am walking in my sleep. Once, I find myself by a ship being unloaded, and the next time, I am surprised to find myself wandering through the marketplace.

Morning becomes afternoon and I am more confused than ever. Coming out was supposed to help me know what to do. But things are worse. Knowing now how they really think of me, I can't live in the palace. But I cannot go to Goshen and become a slave.

I do not recognize that I have wandered full circle back to the new temple until I hear Kakemour call my name. "Mosis!"

At the mere sound of his voice anger surges back into me. I turn around but don't see him.

"Here!"

I see an arm waving to me from the shadows beneath the obelisks at the entrance of the temple. I go up the broad steps and across the porch. I can see now that he is holding someone by the arm, but I cannot tell who it is. As I get closer, I recognize who it is and I want to run away.

Like Abba he has a full beard, only his is night black. I wonder if I would look like him if I grew a beard. I hope he does not recognize me. Why would he? He always avoided me as if I were a crocodile sunning in the middle of the road. Unlike Abba, whose skill is his intelligence, Aharon's hands have an intelligence of their own in the way they can paint a wall and make the figures on them look alive, or carve a ram, a bull, or a calf from the hardest stone and make them so real you are disappointed they are not.

"I've been looking for you," Kakemour says. His lips are smiling, but his eyes are thin with malice.

I try not to look at Aharon. I do not want to know if he knows who I am. But Kakemour makes sure he does.

"It didn't take me long to find your brother. He is known to everyone, as well he should be. He is very talented. Now you will probably think that what I am about to do is cruel. But if you stop and think about it, if you remember all you learned about *maat* from the priests, you would understand that as the son of the *tjat,* as the future *tjat,* as the future son-in-law of the queen and the pharaoh, it is my obligation to be sure that *isfet* is uprooted no matter where it appears."

I know what he is going to ask me to do even before he says it.

"We need to be sure whose side the so-called grandson of the pharaoh is on. Here. Take my whip and use it on your brother. I don't expect you to really hurt him. I'm not a cruel man. I'm not asking you to draw blood. Hit him with the whip. Just once. That's all. It would make such a difference if tonight, at dinner, I could tell Queen Asetnefret that I saw you whip your brother."

Aharon looks at me, but his eyes are expressionless. It is as if he does not know who I am, or maybe worse, does not care that I am his brother. Whatever those eyes are saying, it is clear that they are not afraid and they are not pleading.

Kakemour holds out the short whip he was carrying this morning. Instinctively I take it and am immediately ashamed. What am I doing? I can't strike my own brother. But what would it matter in the long run? I could just touch him lightly with the leather thongs. Aharon would understand. He's practical. And I could make it up to him. Have food sent from the palace for his meal every day, or see that he gets an extra ration of beer. If I don't hit him, I am a traitor to *maat.* Who knows what will happen to me?

I tighten my grip on the whip's smooth wood handle. I imagine drawing back my arm and bringing it down lightly, and then harder and harder. I can almost hear the sound of the leather against bare flesh, can almost see the welts rising on the skin, almost smell the blood trickling through the lacerated flesh.

Then I see the smirk on Kakemour's face and I know! I know what the rest of my life will be like if I whip Aharon. Kakemour will never let me forget I did it. He will never stop asking me to prove my loyalty to the pharaoh. This will not be the end of his testing me but the beginning of something that will never end. Suddenly I remember the first time I saw Almah dance and how the pharaoh stood and applauded her and Kakemour did not. He did not smile even. Suddenly I know, without a doubt, that one day Kakemour will ask me to prove my loyalty by doing something to Almah. He does not know this yet, but when Asetnefret or his new bride see how close the pharaoh and Almah are, they will ask him to do something about "that Habiru priestess" and he will come to me. If I strike my brother now, I will strike my sister then. Or worse.

My arm draws back and before Kakemour realizes what is happening, I am whipping him across the face as hard as I can. His grip on Aharon loosens as he screams in pain and raises his hands to his bleeding face and falls to the ground.

I draw back my arm to strike him again and again, but Aharon knocks the whip from my hand and pushes me away.

"You fool! Now you've made things worse, much worse. Who knows what that Khemetian will do now? He could have us killed, all of us—Ima, Abba, Miryam, and me. And why? All because you were too scared to graze my skin with that whip when he as much as told you that all you had to do was pretend you were whipping me."

Aharon doesn't understand. But he is also right. I have put my family's life in jeopardy.

"Get out of here," he tells me. "I'll stay and help this Khemetian get to a physician. Maybe that will keep him from bringing soldiers to kill us."

I hurry from the temple. I am frightened, yet strangely at peace, too. For the first time in my life, I have done something.

Chapter Six

I HAVE NO CHOICE. I must go to Goshen. I don't dare return to the palace, but I have to tell Almah what has happened. And Mother. But before I do that I want to go back and be sure that Aharon, Abba, Ima, and Miryam are safe. And to tell them that I am coming. I am coming . . . home.

I wander aimlessly, down the side streets near the temple, anxiously waiting for the workday to end and everyone to start for home. I am nervous, even a little frightened but also excited.

Finally the day is ending and people are beginning to leave. When I make my way back to the temple, the Khemetian workers are going slowly up the Street of the Queen to the Workers' Village on the other side of the river.

I look around for Aharon but don't see him. I want to run after the workers and ask them if anything happened this afternoon, if soldiers came and took some Habiru away, but I do not want to draw attention to myself. I can just hope everyone is all right.

I must get back to the palace to see Almah and Mother. Kakemour is already there by now and has told Intef what happened. Soldiers are probably on their way to look for me, and the palace guards will be on the lookout. It will be best if I cross over the Hapi and follow the Avenue of the Crocodiles. More than once I have helped Kakemour get back to the palace that way, stumbling across the sand after the street ends, and sneaking in the back way past the stables and the slaughtering pens.

As I fall in quietly with the Khemetian workers walking toward the village, no one notices as it is not unusual for young noblemen to cross over to their side. The crowds thin quickly as workers disappear down the many side streets to their houses. I continue parallel to the river on the Avenue of the Crocodiles, walking casually as if I have no particular destination in mind but with enough purpose that I appear to know where I am going.

The sun is going down behind me when, two streets ahead, I see a Khemetian nobleman coming out of a side street. I step back quickly and press myself against a house, though when he looks my way, the sun is directly in his eyes. However, because the sun illuminates him, I can see him clearly. It is Kakemour! He turns and goes in the direction I am headed. I don't understand. What's he doing over here? Why isn't he at the palace telling everyone I am a traitor?

When I get to the street out of which he came, I look down it, wondering who could live here that he would have come to see. And then I see the sign: PHYSICIAN. I still don't understand. Why would Kakemour come here to see a doctor when he could be tended to by the Physician to the Pharaoh? Then it comes to me! He doesn't want anyone to know that I beat him with his own whip.

He is going to sneak back into the palace the same way I am planning to. The doctor probably gave him some salves to put on the cuts, and by tomorrow morning his face will not look as bad as it probably does now and he will have thought of some story to tell Intef and no one will ever know what really happened. But he will, which means that one day soon, he will take his revenge on Aharon, Abba, Ima, or Miryam. No. No, he won't. He will find a way to hurt Almah because that will hurt me the most.

I follow him at a safe distance so that if he should happen to look back he would not recognize me. But he only looks straight ahead. As the sun goes lower I know what I have to do. The simple logic of it is almost a relief.

I search the pavement until I find what I am looking for and my hand curls around the large stone. It fits perfectly and grows warm, as if drawing power from deep within me.

We have left the avenue behind and there is now only sand. One is as likely to stumble across a crocodile or snake as someone who has fallen asleep from drinking too much palm wine. No one lives here, and the sandy soil makes it impossible to grow anything.

I move quickly and quietly to close the distance between us. Only when I am almost on him does he hear something or sense my presence and turn around. Recognition comes into his eyes, and as he opens his mouth to say my name, I slam the stone into the side of his head. He drops to the ground like a goose knocked from the sky by a throwing stick. I am about to hit him again when I see that he has not moved.

I bend over to hear if he is breathing. He doesn't seem to be. Taking his wrist, I feel for his pulse. There is none. His eyes are closed, and my fingers feel clumsy as I peel back his eyelid. There is no life in the eye that stares back. He is dead. Kakemour is dead!

I am breathing so heavily that the sound is almost deafening in my ears. My stomach starts cramping, and before I know it I am bending over his body, retching and vomiting so violently I fear I will see my innards pour from my mouth. Eventually, nothing is left to come up. I wipe my mouth with the back of my hand, but the taste of my own filth remains on my tongue and in my throat.

Frantic, I look around but see no one. What am I going to do? I have to bury the body. Taking his ankles, I drag him away from the river and start digging with my hands but the sand keeps sliding back into the hole. Finally, in frustration I throw as much sand over his body as I can and hurry away without looking back.

No one sees me as I slip into the palace grounds and to my suite. I need to sleep. That is all I want to do—go to bed and sleep and wake up to learn that this day was an awful nightmare and tonight Kakemour will take me to a banquet and I will drink palm wine and be very happy.

But when I close my eyes, I see Kakemour's head turning, his eyes meeting mine, his lips beginning to form my name, and after that I remember little. Except that he is dead. Murdered. By me.

The gray of morning comes. I have not slept. I must tell someone. I get up and go to the Women's Palace, hoping Mother has not left for Goshen. I ease myself into her room, and just as she awoke when I was an infant if I so much as turned my head, she awakes now.

"Mosis?"

I go to her, and as I put my arms around her, I start crying as I did not do even as a child. She does not ask me what's wrong but holds me tightly.

Finally my crying slows, then quiets, and I tell her. "I killed Kakemour," I say in a hollow voice. I want to explain but do not know what I would say.

She gasps and I start sobbing again and she hugs me closer, rocking me back and forth, back and forth. This must have been what it was like to be a baby in her arms, and how I wish I could be that again. But I can't. Eventually my sobbing diminishes to an occasional sniffle, and as I watch the light grow brighter and spread across the ceiling and then down the walls, a tear drops onto my hand. Pulling back I see tears covering her face. She utters no sound, but her face is as broken as a bowl that has been knocked off a table. I do not know if she is crying for him or me or because nothing will ever be the same again.

"Sorry," I whisper. "I'm sorry."

She nods, wiping the tears from her face. "I never told you that Kakemour wanted to marry me once."

"Oh, Mother! I . . . I—"

"It's all right. We were not meant for each other. But it is hard to think of him as dead and by the hand of my son. What happened?"

I shake my head. I don't want to talk about it. I don't want to think about it. "I'm sorry," I say again, as if those simple words can undo what cannot be undone.

"I know. Well, we have to do something."

"What?"

"I don't know. Have you told Almah?"

"No."

"We must. I'll see if I can find her. She'll know what to do."

Mother leaves the room, and in a little while she is back.

"Almah is coming."

As we wait in silence, I go over in my mind what happened yesterday, how what was supposed to be a walk into Pi-Ramesses turned into a murder. I know it made sense then. Why doesn't it make sense now? At least sense enough that I could make Mother and Almah understand. Even if I were to tell them that I thought he was going to hurt Almah in some way, did I have to kill him? Then I wonder.

Was it him I was killing, or was it something in myself I wanted dead—my self-loathing for ever thinking of him as my brother, for believing that I mattered to him, my self-hatred for not knowing who I really am. If only I had not gone to Pi-Ramesses yesterday and instead had gone to Goshen and said, *This is my home.* If only.

Almah enters and I tell her.

"Why, Mosis? Why?" she asks, fear and shock flooding her eyes.

I can't tell her. I can't let her see that the person she loves so much is not as wonderful as she thinks.

She turns away to stare at the wall, and I wonder what memories this room holds for her, because she lived here, too, for a little while. Is she remembering all the way back to that first day when she came here with Ima and me? Is she, too, wondering how I got from that day to this?

"What shall we do?" Mother asks softly, breaking the silence.

Almah turns and her eyes catch mine, but I quickly look down at my hands in my lap. "Mosis?"

My head raises involuntarily, and this time her eyes hold me.

"The choice is yours. You can stay here, but that will mean either confessing to Kakemour's murder or living a lie for the rest of your life."

I shake my head. I cannot do either. If I confess, I will probably be killed. And I am not a good liar. The truth would protrude from my face like the snake's head on the pharaoh's headdress. "No. I can't do either."

"Then, you must go to Goshen."

I nod. "I know. Then what? Become a slave?"

"No. I'll think of something."

"Come to Goshen with me?" I ask, knowing the answer but needing to ask the question.

She shakes her head. "I can't. You know that. I'll be all right. Don't worry. Now you must go back to your suite quickly, before too many are about. Late this afternoon you and Batya are to make your way to Ima and Abba's house. Try to sneak out without being seen. I will meet you there after sunset. But do not tell anyone I am coming. If I cannot make it tonight, I will be there as soon as I can. By then I will have figured out what to do next."

WHEN MOTHER AND I arrive in Goshen, everyone is surprised and happy to see me. But Abba and Ima are also puzzled by my visit. Though they do not say anything, I can tell from the way they look at me that they know something is wrong, especially since I am not wearing jewelry or makeup. I am glad they do not ask, but not as glad as I am that Aharon gives me a big hug.

"My brother has returned," he says with a smile. "Forgive me for what I said to you yesterday," he whispers in my ear, holding me close. "I am sorry to say that I was frightened by what you did. Frightened, surprised, and finally, excited. I did not know you cared so much about us. Is that why you are here? Has the Khemetian you whipped threatened you? I was concerned because when we went to work this morning, he was not there."

"What happened after I left? Did you take him to a doctor?"

"I tried to help him, but he told me to get away from him and staggered inside the temple, and that is the last I saw of him."

Ima chatters as she makes supper. I have never heard her talk so much. It does not matter that she talks about nothing. She is happy that I have come home. I wonder how happy she will be when she finds out why.

We eat. Night comes. We sit in the dim light of a lamp. The excitement of my being there has quieted. Now is the time for explanations, but neither Abba nor Ima will ask. They know we are waiting, but for whom or what is not clear until the door opens.

Ima gasps as Almah walks in, but before she can say anything, Almah has crossed the room and is hugging her, tears flowing down her face. Ima's arms make their way around the body of her daughter, and there are tears in her eyes. When they release each other, Almah hugs Aharon, Miryam, and finally, Abba.

There is much sniffling and wiping of eyes, and small bursts of nervous laughter from Almah and Ima. Finally Almah sits on the floor, Ima on one side of her, Mother on the other. I look at them, my three mothers, together in the same room, side by side.

"Have you told them?" Almah asks me.

I shake my head, not wanting to remember why I am here.

"What's the matter?" Ima wants to know.

"Mosis killed the son of the *tjat,* the man who was going to marry one of the daughters of Asetnefret and himself be *tjat* one day," Almah says matter-of-factly.

"What?" Abba asks, shocked.

"He killed a Khemetian," Ima says with pleasure in her voice. "An important Khemetian, it sounds like."

"Why, Mosis?" Abba asks in a pained voice.

"The Khemetians offend Ya. That's reason enough," Ima interjects.

"No, it isn't," Almah answers calmly, "but there isn't time for this. Mosis, Kakemour's body was found this afternoon. Because no one has seen you since yesterday, Ramesses wonders if you were killed also. Intef, however, wonders if you aren't the killer and have come here to hide. Ramesses is sending soldiers in the morning to look for you."

"What shall I do? No basket big enough this time."

Almah smiles sadly. "No. There isn't. There is no place in Khemet where you would not be found. You have to go."

I look at her, shock, disbelief, and panic coming into my eyes with such rapidity that I am ashamed. "What?"

"You cannot stay in Goshen and you cannot stay in Khemet. If you want to live." I hear a catch in Almah's voice as she says the last.

"I don't believe this," I manage to say. I look around at them—Abba, Ima, Mother, Aharon, Miryam, and Almah—my eyes pleading. They look back, Ima and Mother with tears in their eyes, but no one's eyes answer my plea.

"Why?" I say angrily. "No one saw."

"I'm not sure," Almah says. "Just because you saw no one doesn't mean you weren't seen. As I was leaving the palace tonight, I was stopped by a servant. He was not Habiru, but he spoke Habiru. He told me that he overheard two Habiru saying they had seen the Habiru who dresses like a Khemetian following someone as they left the temple yesterday."

"That's a lie!"

"Mosis!" It is Abba. "I am ashamed of you. Almah is risking her life by being here tonight."

I drop my head and then look up. "Forgive me," I say to Almah. "I . . . I am afraid. I don't know where to go. And what will I do once I get somewhere? I hadn't planned on any of this."

"No, but Ya did," Ima interjects. "All these years I have told myself that Ya took you to live among idolaters because he had great plans for you. Now I understand. What you have done, my son, is good! You killed a Khemetian! You could do that only because you have known something we don't. Freedom! You know what it feels like to be free! Free! Growing up as the pharaoh's grandson, you have breathed nothing but freedom. Since the death of Yosef, no Habiru has been free—until you. You must go and come back and teach us all to be free."

I nod my head slowly, though right now I do not feel free.

Almah gets up from the floor. "I'm sorry I have to go so soon," she says, hugging Ima again, then everyone else. "But it is time for Mosis to leave."

"What . . . what is your plan, Almah?"

Everyone looks at Ima. It is the first time in my life I have heard that name pass her lips. Almah is startled, too, and she blinks her eyes rapidly to hold back the tears.

"It is better if you don't know, Ima. Then, when the soldiers come tomorrow and ask where Mosis is, you can say truthfully that you don't know."

Ima smiles and nods her agreement. There is nothing else to do but hug everyone, to look at them and try to impress their faces on my mind, as I will never see them again. Most difficult of all is leaving Mother. She is sobbing uncontrollably, and now it is my turn to hold her as if she were a baby. As I do so, I feel that everything will be all right. I don't know how. But it will.

"Come. We must hurry."

I wipe Mother's tears from her face with my hands and, giving her one last hug, follow Almah into the darkness.

YEAR 30 OF THE REIGN OF RAMESSES THE GREAT, 2ND MONTH OF AKHET, DAY 22

Epilogue

I GET UP WHEN I SEE the blackness on the ceiling change to gray. I do not know how long I have been awake. Sometimes I wonder if I have slept at all since Mosis left. The emptiness inside me seems as deep and unending as the blackness of night. I understand now why Batya cried so much when Nefertari died. I did not know my body held so many tears.

I don't cry as much now as I did the first month. Then it was all through the night, every night. I do not cry as often now or for as long a period of time, but I feel raw inside, as if my heart were hanging from a tree.

It is light enough to see the dim outlines of the feathers on Eset's wings on the wall painting across from my bed. If I did not have the goddesses to serve, I would have died. No, that is not true. If not for the goddesses, I would have gone with him. I almost did that night. As we made our way out of Goshen, I began thinking that I would never see him again, that he would never again be waiting for me at the end of my day, that I would never sit and share silence with him. He will never know how close I came to saying, *I will come with you.*

But I couldn't, not when I thought about what the reaction would be when both Mosis and I could not be found. I was not sure how the pharaoh would respond when he realized Mosis was gone. But if we were both missing he would send soldiers as far as Syria to find us. My staying was Mosis's best protection.

I had to stay also because if I leave Khemet, my *ka* will die. This is where I have to be in order to be myself. No matter how much I miss Mosis, it would be far more awful to live with eternal longing for myself. And so I watched the darkness swallow him just as it swallows the sun each evening. But we have the pharaoh to make the sun return each morning. There is no one who can make Mosis return. Ima insists that Ya will send him back when Ya has made him ready. If Mosis were to come back, I think I would be convinced that Ya is more powerful than all the other gods.

I pour water into a bowl and wash my hands three times and then put water lightly on my face in order to make a separation between my night self and the me who is coming into being with the new day. Then I go out into the hallway.

The palace is completely still. My bare feet do not make a sound on the tiled floors as I make my way toward the stairs to the roof. As I pass the suite of rooms where Mosis lived, I try not to think that the daughter of Asetnefret who was to have married Kakemour lives there now. I try not to think or remember much these days.

When I reach the roof, the eastern sky is tinged with dark blue. To the north, in Goshen, Abba and Aharon stand on a roof looking at the same sky. I hope that somewhere on the other side of the desert Mosis is also looking at this sky.

It has been almost six weeks since I made it seem that the mules had broken from their pen so Mosis could ride away on one into the desert. The servants spent much of the following morning trying to catch the mules, and in so doing, their footprints obliterated those of the one mule that carried weight on its back. Though I overheard speculation about how the mules got out, no one suspected the truth.

I sit down and, crossing my legs, I close my eyes and begin breathing deeply and slowly. I focus on the ingoing and outgoing of my breath, shedding my mind's desire to indulge in useless speculations about whether he is alive and where he might be. I have no other awareness than that of my breath, in which is my life and my *ka*. This is who I am, this breath, this life, this *ka*.

"In peace, my daughter."

Ramesses's voice startles me. I turn my head. He has not yet put on eye makeup or a wig, and his baldness gives him the appearance of even more strength than he normally has. He is wearing only a kilt, and I can see the stubble of hair on his legs, indicating that he has not been shaved yet.

"I did not mean to startle you," he continues.

"That's all right," I say, unable to hide the apprehension in my voice. Why is he here? It must be urgent because no one is permitted to see him without a wig on. Has he come to tell me that they have caught Mosis, or that his body was found in the desert? I start to get up, but he motions me to remain seated and comes to sit beside me.

"Relax. I knew I would find you here. I wanted to talk without other ears about. We have not talked, father to daughter and daughter to father, since the murder, and the disappearance of Mosis."

I am not sure I want to know what he is hinting at, but my face remains expressionless. Though I am with him each day, it is after he has dressed. Seeing him thus, I am surprised by the weariness in his eyes, at the shadow of age hovering over him.

He smiles. "After all these years I still look at you and see her. I don't know how I would have survived if I had not had you. I wanted to marry you, you know, and would have, but you never seemed interested. Did you know?"

I nod. "A woman knows when a man's desires are reaching for her, even when she is twelve."

"And how does that feel?"

"It depends. On the man. Sometimes it is flattering. Sometimes it is intrusive. And sometimes it is elevating."

"And how did my desire for you feel?"

"Elevating but intrusive," I respond simply. "I knew I was not her. If I had let you marry me, you would have been more aware of what had been taken from you, not what had been given."

"Perhaps, but you could have been Queen of Khemet.

Isn't that what every woman wants?" He says this last with a touch of sarcasm.

"I am a better daughter and priestess than wife, yours or any man's."

He nods. "Only when I saw that you desired no man, none except your brother, was I able to let you be."

The sky is white where the sun has risen. I should have begun my morning prayers already. However, it is not every day that the pharaoh wants to talk to you.

"You and your mother speak now?" he asks, after a long pause.

I am surprised, but little happens in Khemet that Ramesses does not know. "Yes. Yes, we do. I visit every week or so. We have agreed that she can talk to me about Ya, but I will not speak of Eset or Hathor to her."

He chuckles. "A wise decision, I would think."

"I don't mind. Mainly, though, we talk about how hard life is now. She wants to know why you have become cruel to the Habiru. Because everyone now works from sun to sun, they do not have time to tend their gardens, and the food you have provided for them is not enough. Women, children, and old people die every day from the hard work and from accidents. This is not like you."

He looks sharply at me and I wonder if I have crossed a boundary, but his face softens. "I should have made you *tjat.* You are not afraid of me. But you know the answer to your question. The Habiru disturb *maat.* They have been in Khemet for more than two hundred years, and yet, they still live as strangers among us. They keep to themselves. They will not eat with us. They will not socialize with us. They refuse to learn our language. This goes against the divine order. The hard labor I have imposed on them is the only way I can protect *maat*."

"You could let them go free."

"That would disturb *maat* most of all. It would seem like I was rewarding them for their defiance of the divine order. Let their Ya come and free them. I won't. And speaking of Ya, how is the daughter of god?"

There is a tinge of sarcasm in his voice, but I ignore it. "Batya is well. She is the daughter Ima always wanted."

"Don't you have a sister?"

"Miryam. She's a little odd. Like me. I am getting to know her. The other day she asked me what it feels like to dance."

"Does the daughter of god ever ask about me?"

"No. She is angry, and she is ashamed of what you are doing to the Habiru."

"And you?" he asks, looking at me with those eyes one cannot lie to.

"I am sorry to say that I understand. I believe in *maat*. But I don't like what you have done."

"I'm not sorry you feel that way. Asetnefret and Intef derive too much pleasure from what I am doing to the Habiru. I have none. I do what I do because I am the guardian of Khemet."

"I will tell Batya what you said."

"Thank you. Tell her, also, that I miss her."

Half of the sun's disk is above the horizon now, and

the clear sky seems to be inhaling the light. I am enjoying talking with Ramesses, but I also wish he would go so I could greet the day.

"I had a visitor a week or so ago," he says too casually. "A Syrian. It seems that he had just come from the land of Midian, where he stayed a few days with a priest named Yitro. Living in Yitro's house was a young man who spoke Khemetian."

My facial expression does not change, but my heart feels like it stops beating.

"What was odd, the traveler said, was that the young Khemetian was not a runaway servant or slave. He had the bearing of one from the nobility. I'm sure the traveler would have said more, but I showed no curiosity and he went on to talk about other things. But I sent my son Merenptah to investigate. He returned and confirmed what I thought was the case. Please tell your mother I regret that I cannot ease her physical burden, but perhaps it will lighten her *ka*—and yours—to know that Mosis is alive and well."

I cannot restrain myself, and I throw my arms around his neck and hug him tightly. "Thank you. Thank you." Although it is forbidden to touch the pharaoh, I have always been the exception, besides his wives and concubines, of course.

"Did Mosis kill Kakemour?"

That is like Ramesses, to ask what he really wants to know when you are feeling most tender toward him. I sit back. "Yes."

"Why?"

"I asked him that. He would not say at first, but finally, just . . . just before he left, he needed me to know. He was angry that you did not want him to leave the palace grounds until after the temple was finished, that you no longer trusted him."

"How did he know this?"

"That is what both Intef and Kakemour told him. It seems that Kakemour decided to test Mosis's loyalty to you by trying to make Mosis beat his brother, Aharon, with a whip. Instead Mosis used the whip on Kakemour. Mosis was afraid Kakemour would try to take his revenge on me, and to protect me, Mosis felt he had no choice but to murder Kakemour."

Ramesses is quiet for a long time. "It is too bad Mosis did not come and ask me."

"Why is that?" I ask, confused.

"I gave no orders for Mosis to be confined to the palace grounds."

"You didn't?" I am shocked.

"No. Do you really think I was afraid Mosis would foment rebellion among the Habiru? Mosis had my trust far more than he knew. I was not happy at the thought of Kakemour becoming *tjat* and my son-in-law. That was putting too much power at Asetnefret's disposal. I was going to make Mosis *tjat* after the wedding. I would not be surprised if Kakemour sensed my displeasure with him and tried to provoke Mosis, thus giving Kakemour an excuse to kill him. He underestimated Mosis's intelligence and courage, and now he is dead."

I am stunned. Mosis as *tjat.* It would not have worked. Perhaps Ya knew that Mosis had to leave Khemet, and the murder of Kakemour was the only way that could be arranged.

"And you? Did you help Mosis escape?"

I was not expecting this question, either. I want to tell him no. I have never done anything he would disapprove of—except that. But to lie would hurt him more than the truth. "Yes."

He nods. "When I heard that Kakemour had been murdered, I was shocked. We do not have murders in Khemet. Nothing disturbs *maat* so greatly as murder. Then I heard Mosis was missing, and I feared he had been murdered, too. But Intef and Asetnefret thought otherwise, especially because the mules so mysteriously broke out of their pen—and one has not yet been found. I knew then that they were right, though I did not tell them. I wanted to send soldiers after him and have him brought back so I could kill him myself. But I could not have done that. Have Mosis executed? I loved him more than many of my own sons. So, better that he not be caught. Then there is nothing I have to do. There is nothing I have to admit. I know where he is. I know he is well. That is enough.

"Incidentally, both Asetnefret and Intef were convinced you helped Mosis escape. I thought that was probably so, too. But when you appeared the morning after Kakemour's body was discovered and expressed your grief to Asetnefret and Intef, they did not know what to think. I saw the tension in your face, and I admire your being able to hold it all within—the murder, the loss of your brother, the need to help him escape, and above all, your loyalty to me, to the gods, to Khemet. As long as I live, Asetnefret will not harm you. And I expect to outlive her by many years." He laughs softly.

"Now I apologize. I have kept you from your morning prayers. I know the priests restrict you to the service of Eset and Hathor." He chuckles. "And well they should. If you were to start doing other rituals, they would be out of jobs. Though you are forbidden to sing the Hymn to Osiris, I have no doubt that you know it."

I smile. "Of course."

"You will sing it for me?"

I rise. The sun's disk is almost entirely above the horizon now. If I were alone I would remove my dress and stand naked to receive the new day and the new life it brings into my being. But I do not want to awaken desire in Ramesses. And then I think, no, I cannot let his presence alter the way I pray. Let his eyes and mind do what they will. This morning of all mornings my heart bursts with the need to thank the gods for keeping Mosis safe.

I remove my dress, and the sun covers my body with its soft warmth. I close my eyes and throw back my head until my face is parallel with the sky. Then slowly I raise my arms straight up from my body, and then lower them until they are even with my shoulders and draw them in front of my body, palms upraised, and I sing:

"Greetings to you, Osiris, Lord of eternity, King of the gods.
Your names are many; your forms are holy.
For you the waters are poured out.
For you the winds approach at evening.
The heights of heaven and the stars obey you.
He makes the mighty gates to open before him, Osiris,
Who is praised in the southern heaven
And adored in the northern heaven.
The never-setting stars are under his rule
And his abodes are the stars that never rest.
He has set his fear in all lands, and
Through their love for him,
They exalt his name above every other name.
All nations praise him and with one voice
Utter cries of joy. With his hand
He made this earth, and the water, air,
Vegetation, cattle, feathered fowl, fishes,
Creeping things, and beasts of all kinds.
He rises in the horizon. He lightens the darkness.
He floods the Two Lands with splendor in the early morning.
He is gracious in speech.
He is the favored one of the gods."

As the sound of the hymn dies, I open my eyes. Through my tears I see that the full disk of the sun rests on the edge of the world. Somewhere in the land of Midian, my brother Mosis is looking at the same disk.

I put on my dress and turn to look at Ramesses. I am surprised to see tears in his eyes.

"How do you say it in Habiru?" he asks. *"Hallelu Ya?"*

I am startled. All these years I have known him, and I did not know he knew any Habiru.

He smiles. "I have been trying to learn what I can, should that be the only language Batya will use with me—if I ever see her again."

I offer him my hand and help him get up. "Yes. *Hallelu Ya,"* I say. Praise God.

As we start down the steps to go inside and begin the new day, I stop and look at the sun. The god has survived another journey through the chaos of night. And so has Mosis.

So has Mosis.

Author's Note

THE NOVEL DEVELOPED far differently than I had anticipated. This was due primarily to the extensive research I did about ancient Egypt. What I learned was that the negative picture of Egypt given in the book of Exodus is not historically accurate. While it may reflect how the ancient Hebrew *felt* about the Egyptians, it distorts Egyptian civilization and culture. As I read and watched videos about ancient Egypt, I knew that I did not want to write a novel in which the Jews were the good guys and the Egyptians the bad. Human experience is more complex than that.

The challenge with any novel is how to tell the story. Which voice or voices will best communicate the time, the place, the people? I tried different points of view and voices—third person omniscient, first person using Batya—but neither worked. Then I wondered, *What about telling it from the point of view of Miriam, the sister of Moses who watches the basket in which the baby Moses is lying and offers to get a wet nurse for the baby after Pharaoh's daughter discovers it?*

I went back to the book of Exodus to reread the story and, to my surprise, found that Miriam is not mentioned. "Then said his sister to Pharaoh's daughter: 'Shall I go and call you a nurse of the Hebrew women, that she may nurse the child for you?' And Pharaoh's daughter said to her: 'Go.' And the maiden went and called the child's mother." (Exodus 2:7–9)

I looked in a concordance and found that Miriam is not mentioned by name until the crossing of the Red Sea: "And Miriam the prophetess, the sister of Aaron, took a timbrel in her hand; and all the women went out after her with timbrels and with dances. And Miriam sang to them. . . ." (Exodus 15:20–21) Rabbinic exegetical tradition does not like people in the Torah to be nameless and bestows names or links people from different stories. Thus, finding a name for a sister in this story, the rabbis assumed it was the same sister who offered to get a nurse for her baby brother.

I did not make that assumption. Instead I asked myself, *Why didn't the Torah call Miriam by name from the beginning?* I reread Exodus 2:8, this time in Hebrew: "Va'tomer lah bat-Paro lechi va-telech ha-almah va-tikra et-aim ha-yeled." ("And the daughter of Pharaoh said to her, 'Go,' and the young girl of marriageable age went and called the mother of the child.")

When I read the word *almah,* "a young girl of marriageable age," the thought came: *What if Moses had a sister older than Miriam named Almah?* I knew I had the character and the voice through whom the story could be told.

Writing about a civilization that existed more than three thousand years ago is a challenge, to put it mildly. Yet, because the Egyptians left a visual record in the numerous tomb paintings as well as written records, we know a lot about ancient Egypt. All the names used are authentic, and I have sought to be historically faithful throughout and in ways that will not always be obvious. For example, ancient Egyptians had no concept of time smaller than an hour. That is why no character here says, "Wait a minute," and there are no descriptions saying, "She paused for an instant." (At least I hope that is the case. It is very difficult to write without measuring time as we are accustomed to doing.) The Egyptians did not have money, so I could not have a character ask, "How did you spend your day?" or use figures of speech using concepts involving payment, such as "He paid a price for what he did."

For those who might be bothered by the references to nudity, nudity was common in ancient Egypt. I did not include it to the extent that I could have, for fear that extensive inclusion would overshadow the book itself. Too, I was not writing a history book. This is a novel. As such, it is ultimately a work of the imagination. No one knows for sure what happened more than three thousand years ago when a people we call Egyptians and a people we call Hebrews encountered each other. We have the story as recorded in a sacred text, but sacred texts record sacred truths, not necessarily historical ones. My concern here is not sacred truths but human and psychological ones.

And human and psychological truths can illuminate sacred truth, revealing dimensions and facets that cannot be seen in any other way.

A word about how I have portrayed Moses: Besides the Torah, our ideas about who Moses was have been given to us by popular culture, namely two films, Cecil B. DeMille's epic *The Ten Commandments*, with Charlton Heston as Moses and Yul Brynner as Ramesses, and the animated film *Prince of Egypt*. Both depict Moses and Ramesses as brothers, and both also depict Moses as growing up and learning only later that he is Hebrew.

Historians believe that Ramesses the Great was the pharaoh referred to in the Torah. I decided to make him Moses' grandfather rather than his brother because the Torah also tells us that the Hebrews "built for Pharaoh store-cities, Pithom and Raamses." (Exodus 1:11) If the city named Raamses—Pi-Ramesses in Egyptian (House of Ramesses)—was built by the Hebrews before the birth of Moses, I concluded that Ramesses the Great was already on the throne and, therefore, could not have grown up with Moses as his brother.

The novel also reflects my long held view that Moses was the first person in history to grow up with a split identity, and attempts to resolve it through an act of violence. In my imagination Moses always knew he was Hebrew, but he loved being Egyptian. There is some confirmation for this in the Torah. When Moses flees Egypt and goes to the land of Midian, the daughters of the priest of Midian go to their father and say, "An Egyptian delivered us out of the hand of the shepherds. . . ."

(Exodus 2:19) Obviously, then, Moses looked like an Egyptian and may even have identified himself to the daughters as an Egyptian. The Midrash says that one reason God did not permit Moses to enter the Promised Land or even be buried there was because he pretended to be an Egyptian when he went into Midian.

The toughest problem to resolve was Moses' speech. In translations Moses is described as a stutterer. But in the Hebrew, he describes himself as being "heavy of mouth and heavy of tongue." No one knows exactly what this means, but in Hebrew there are times when Moses' speech differs from occasions when he is repeating what God has told him to say. Sometimes when Moses is speaking for himself, the Hebrew has an almost primitive quality, a heaviness of mouth and tongue that is difficult to convey in English. One of the ironies of the Moses story is that the man God chooses to be the deliverer is also a man who has difficulty speaking. This detail adds a human dimension to the figure of Moses, which I have tried to convey through what sometimes sounds like pidgin English. One will not see Charlton Heston in my Moses.

One of the major problems in writing historical fiction is that of how did people talk? What distinctions existed between informal and formal speech? What were the colloquialisms and figures of speech? Often historical fiction errs in one of two ways—either the language is so stilted and formal that it bears little resemblance to an English that the reader can see himself in, or it disregards history entirely and uses modern slang that also distances the reader from the book. I have sought the middle ground by varying the formality and informality of language depending on who is talking and to whom. I am grateful to Professor David Van Blerkom, a colleague of mine at the University of Massachusetts who teaches astronomy and from time to time offers a seminar in hieroglyphs. He confirmed my sense that while the written Egyptian of sacred texts is formal, the spoken language was, for the most part, informal.

The "Hymn to Osiris" at the end of the novel is adapted from "Hymn to Osiris" in E. A. Wallis Budge's *The Dwellers on the Nile* (see the bibliography). I want to acknowledge Professor Helen Lefkowitz of the Classics Department of Wellesley College, whose e-mail correspondence, suggestions of books, collegiality, and responses to my questions and speculations were helpful during the research phase of this book. However, she does not share responsibility for any historical errors that may be found herein.

I also want to thank Rabbi Yechiael Lander, the now retired Jewish chaplain at Smith and Amherst Colleges. Back in 1979 when I spontaneously found myself writing about Bythia, the daughter of Pharaoh, I wondered if what I was writing was violating Jewish tradition. So I took what I had written to Rabbi Lander who, after reading it, smiled and explained, "This is midrash."—a way of exploring a text through the use of one's imagination. It is a time-honored tradition in Judaism. Rather than violating Jewish tradition, I was exemplifying it. Two years later Rabbi Lander would supervise my conversion to Judaism.

A warm thanks to my editor, Paula Wiseman, and her assistant, Rachel Goldberg, and everyone at Harcourt. You are a joy to work with.

Without the presence in my life of Milan Sabatini, my wife, best friend, companion, researcher, and at-home editor, neither I nor this book would be.

A final note: Like many people, I am not sure if I believe in reincarnation. But I have always found it interesting how people can be drawn to certain periods in history and not others. Ancient Greece and Rome have always bored me, whereas ancient Egypt feels like home in a deep sense. So, in writing this novel and feeling that I was writing my own story (in my identification with Almah), I couldn't help wonder if in a previous life I had lived in the time of Ramesses the Great.

Several months after finishing the novel, I was reading to my wife one evening as she lay in bed, a custom of ours. One of the books we are reading is the *Oxford English Dictionary*—all twenty volumes! On this particular evening I came to a word and, literally, chills went through me, leaving me unable to speak for several moments. Finally, still unable to speak, I slid the volume to my wife and let her read it for herself. The word was *almah*: "An Egyptian dancing-girl."

Glossary

PRACTICALLY ALL of our vocabulary regarding ancient Egypt, including the word *Egypt,* comes to us from either the Greeks or the Arabs. Where possible I have substituted the original Egyptian words for place names, months, deities, etc. I have also used Hebrew names for the more familiar English ones. As readers we bring our own historical and cultural contexts to what we read. Imagining oneself into history–as readers and writers—challenges us to leave behind as many of our associations as we can in an effort to understand the past, and in doing so, better understand ourselves. It is an act of respect we hope will be shown us when we are someone else's past. —J. L.

Abba Hebrew for Father

Aharon Hebrew for Aaron

Akhet Name of one of the three Egyptian seasons. Akhet was the Season of the Inundation when the Nile flooded. It corresponds to the months of July through October.

Amon-Re The primary deity of Egypt during the New Kingdom (1550–1070 B.C.E.)

Amram The name given to the father of Moses by Jewish tradition.

Amu Egyptian word for Hyksos, Asiatic peoples who lived in Egypt from 1640 to 1532 B.C.E. They introduced military weapons and the horse and chariot to Egyptian culture, and revolutionized agricultural methods.

Asetnefret The actual name of the Second Royal Wife of Ramses. Her name is also sometimes spelled as Isetnefret.

Avraham Hebrew for Abraham

Battle of Kadesh A battle between a Hittite army and an Egyptian army led by Ramses the Great that resulted in a treaty between the two kingdoms. The courage and leadership Ramses showed in battle did much to establish his reputation among his own people.

Batya Hebrew name for Bythia, the daughter of Pharaoh who took the baby Moses from the Nile River and raised him as her son

Book of the Dead An ancient Egyptian book that gave instructions on how to survive in the afterlife to the deceased. These instructions were placed on the walls of tombs.

Chava Hebrew for Eve

Esav Hebrew for Esau

Eset The Egyptian goddess we know by her Greek name, Isis

Festival of Opet A New Year's festival held at the time the Nile flooded. It lasted for a month and was held at present-day Karnak and Luxor.

Gan Eden Hebrew for the Garden of Eden

Goshen The name of the region of Egypt where the Hebrews lived, as written in the Torah. See Genesis 47:4.

Great Green Sea A translation of the Egyptian name for the Mediterranean Sea

Great Hapi Egyptian name for the Nile. It means "sweet water."

Habiru The ancient Akkadian name for the Hebrew people. Since there is no reference in ancient Egyptian records to the children of Israel, it is impossible to know how they were referred to in Egyptian. I chose an ancient word that was used for them. It is also spelled sometimes as Hapiru. The etymology is unclear, but it is possible that from this word came the Hebrew word *ivri,* "people from the other side," which is used in the Torah.

Hathor Egyptian goddess who was the protector of women and patron of love and joy and mistress of song and dance

Hittites An ancient people who lived in an area that is now Anatolia, Turkey, and northern Syria

Hor The Egyptian god Horus

Hor-em-akhet Egyptian name for the Sphinx

Ima Hebrew for Mother (pronounced Eee-mah)

isfet In Egyptian religion, the concept of injustice, violence, and chaos with which *maat* was in a constant battle to defeat

ka An Egyptian word with several layers of meaning: (1) the spiritual essence of a person that was the guiding force of life; (2) an astral being that existed alongside a person and had its own individuality; (3) an aspect of the divine essence on which all existence depended

Kakemour This is an ancient Egyptian male name. The character is invented.

Khemet What the Egyptians called Egypt. It means "black land" because of the mud deposited by the annual inundations of the Nile. Upper Egypt, where the Nile is bordered on both sides by desert, was known as Red Land.

Maat Both a goddess and the ancient Egyptian spiritual ideal. It is similar to the Taoist concept of Tao, denoting cosmic balance and harmony between earth, heaven, and humanity.

Merenptah The fourteenth son of Ramses the Great; he became coruler during the latter years of Ramses's reign and succeeded him as pharaoh.

Meryetamun One of the daughters of Ramses the Great and Nefertari. A statue of her is found at Abu Simbel, the temple built to mark the thirtieth year of Ramses's reign.

Miryam Hebrew for Miriam

Mosis Scholars agree that the biblical name Moses is a shortened form of an ancient Egyptian name, as in Tuthmosis. It is believed that the prefix of Moses' name was lost.

Nefertari First Great Royal Wife of Ramses the Great. She was reputed to be a woman of extraordinary beauty and character. She died at about the thirtieth year of Ramses's reign. We know of his great love for her because of the statues of her at Abu Simbel. It was rare for a pharaoh to depict any of his wives. Also, Ramses had a temple built in her honor next to his own at Abu Simbel. Her tomb at Thebes is one of the most well preserved, and the wall paintings showing her are among the most remarkable tomb paintings that have survived.

Opet Today known as the city of Thebes

Osiris	One of the central gods of ancient Egypt
Pi-Ramesses	The city built by Ramses the Great in the delta. It is referred to in the Torah in Exodus 1:11: "Therefore they did set over them taskmasters to afflict them with their burdens. And they built for Pharaoh store-cities, Pithom and Raamses." No ruins of the city remain, and its location is uncertain.
Ra'kha'ef	Pharaoh who reigned from 2520 to 2494 B.C.E. and built the second pyramid and the Sphinx at Giza
Ramesses II	Also known as Ramses the Great (1290–1224 B.C.E.) The longest reigning pharaoh, who lived to age 96 and is believed to have had more than 200 wives and concubines and sired 96 sons and 60 daughters. Some scholars believed he is the Pharaoh of the Bible.
Rivka	Hebrew for Rebecca
Sarah	Wife of Avraham
Season of the Inundation	See Akhet.
Shemu	The season of Harvest, corresponding to the months of March through June
shesheset	(Also known as *sistrum* or *seses*) Musical instrument associated with the goddess Hathor
Sutekh	The god Seth. The Egyptian name means "instigator of confusion," "the destroyer."
Taweret	The goddess of childbirth who was depicted with the body of a hippopotamus, the head of a crocodile or lion, and the feet of a lion. She was sometimes dressed in the robes of a queen.
tjat	"The robed one," or prime minister, as we would say today

Wadjet Goddess who was the protector of Lower Egypt

Ya One of the Hebrew names of God. The English word *hallelujah* is the anglicization of the Hebrew *hallelu*, "praise," *Ya*, "God."

Yaakov Hebrew for Jacob

Yekutiel According to Jewish tradition, the name Moses was given at birth.

Yitzchak Hebrew for Isaac

Yocheved According to Jewish tradition, the name of the mother of Moses

Bibliography

BOOKS

Andrews, Carol. *Amulets of Ancient Egypt.* London: British Museum Press, 1994.

———. *Ancient Egyptian Jewelry.* London: British Museum Press, 1990.

Baines, John, and Jaromír Malék. *Atlas of Ancient Egypt.* New York: Facts on File Publications, 1996.

Barbarian Tides: TimeFrame 1500–600 B.C. Alexandria, Va.: Time-Life Books, 1987.

Budge, E. Wallis. *The Dwellers of the Nile: The Life, History, Religion, and Literature of the Ancient Egyptians.* New York: Dover, 1977.

Bunson, Margaret R. *A Dictionary of Ancient Egypt.* New York: Oxford University Press, 1995.

Gillispie, Charles Coulston, and Michel Dewachter, eds. *Monuments of Egypt: The Napoleonic Edition.* 2 vols. Princeton, N.J.: Princeton Architectural Press, in association with the Architectural League of New York and the J. Paul Getty Trust, 1987.

Hobson, Christine. *The World of the Pharaohs: A Complete Guide to Ancient Egypt.* New York: Thames and Hudson, 1987.

Kunz, George Frederick. *Curious Lore of Precious Stones.* New York: Dover, 1971.

Maitland, Sara. *The Ancient Egyptian Pack and Book.* Illustrated by Christos Kondeatis. Boston: Bulfinch Press, 1996.

McDonald, John K. *House of Eternity: The Tomb of Nefertari.* Los Angeles: Getty Conservation Institute and J. Paul Getty Museum, 1996.

Montet, Pierre. *Everyday Life in Egypt in the Days of Ramesses the Great.* Philadelphia: University of Pennsylvania Press, 1958.

Murnane, William J. *The Penguin Guide to Ancient Egypt.* London: Penguin, 1983.

Past Worlds: The London Times Atlas of Archaeology. New York: Crescent Books, 1995.

Patrick, Richard. *All Colour Book of Egyptian Mythology.* London: Octopus Books Ltd., 1972.

Reeves, Nicholas. *The Complete Tutankhamun.* New York: Thames and Hudson, 1990.

Robins, Gay. *Women in Ancient Egypt.* Cambridge, Mass.: Harvard University Press, 1993.

Scamuzzi, Ernesto. *Egyptian Art in the Egyptian Museum of Turin.* New York: Harry N. Abrams (no date).

Scholz, Piotr O. *Ancient Egypt: An Illustrated Historical Overview.* Hauppauge, N.Y.: Barrons Educational Series, 1997.

Stead, Miriam. *Egyptian Life.* Cambridge, Mass.: Harvard University Press, 1986.

Steedman, Scott. *Ancient Egypt.* New York: DK Publishing, 1995.

Tyldesley, Joyce. *Daughters of Isis: Women of Ancient Egypt.* New York: Viking Penguin, 1995.

Unstead, R. J. *See Inside an Egyptian Town.* London: Kingfisher Books Ltd., 1986.

Yoyotte, Jean. *Treasures of the Pharaohs.* Geneva: Skira, 1968.

What Life Was Like on the Banks of the Nile: Egypt 3050–30 B.C. Alexandria, Va.: Time-Life Books, 1996.

PERIODICALS

Arden, Harvey. "In Search of Moses." *National Geographic* (January 1976): 2–37.

Dothan, Trude. "Lost Outpost of the Egyptian Empire." *National Geographic* (December 1982): 739–769.

Gore, Rick. "Ramses the Great." *National Geographic* (April 1991): 2–31.
Johnson, Electa and Irving. "*Yankee* Cruises the Storied Nile." *National Geographic* (May 1965): 583–633.
Kendall, Timothy. "Kingdom of Kush." *National Geographic* (November 1990): 96–125.
Miller, Peter. "Riddle of the Pyramid Boats." *National Geographic* (April 1988): 534–550.
Roberts, David. "Age of Pyramids: Egypt's Old Kingdom." *National Geographic* (January 1995): 2–43.
Simpich, Frederick. "Along the Nile, Through Egypt and the Sudan." *National Geographic* (October 1922): 379–410.

VIDEOCASSETTES

The Giant Nile. Blue Bird Films, 1990.
The Great Pharaohs of Egypt. A&E Television Networks, 1997.

WEB PAGES

Ancient Egyptian Virtual Temple. http://www.netins.net/showcase/ankh/index.html
Encarta Interactive World Atlas Online. http://www.encarta.com/ewa/pages/a/42297.htm
Tour Egypt. http://touregypt.com
The Great Temple of Abu Simbel. http://www.ccer.ggl.ruu.nl/abu_simbel
University of Chicago Epigraphic Survey. http://www-oi.uchicago.edu/OI/Mus/PA/EGYPT/Egypt_AbuSimbel.html